The Billionaire's Dark Secrets

Charlotte Reagan

Contents

Chapter 1

Anusha POV:

This night is very cold, there was snow all around and I was running on the snow in bare feet. I had to escape from the man who had ruined my life by whatever means possible.

I wanted to run away to the furthest place where he couldn't catch me. I thought the man was like my father but he turned out to be a beast.

I know that he is chasing me and i cannot run away from him. There is no one of mine in this country.But yes i can hide from him as much as i can.

I was missing my Dad and Mother alot. If they were alive, all this would not have happened.

I was running and then i saw a garden and i went inside that garden and hide behind a big tree.

Suddenly i heard someone calling my name.

Anuuuushaaa....Babyydolll...come outside. You know you can't hide from me. Just come outside my babydoll. - he said while laughing like a monster.

My heart skipped a beat after hearing his voice. I start sobbing silently. He heard my crying and he caught me.

Leave me.. Please leave me alone. I'm just like your daughter. My dad trusted you that you will raise me like your daughter. He gave my responsibility to you before he took his last breath.i said while crying hardly.

He laugh like a beast and said- But I didn't know that this responsibility would grow and become soo beautiful.

I am just 15 year old. Please leave me alone. You can't do this to me - i said crying.

He grabbed me by force and lifted me on his shoulder and started walking towards home. I was crying and screaming for help. But i know there is nobody here to help me.

He took me back home. And he threw me on the bed.He started taking off his clothes. And jumped over me. I was struggling so hard. This makes him angry. Then he slapped me so hard on my face. I left numb at that moment. I was started loosing my consciousness at that moment but he didn't stop. He rapped me.

Suddenly my Alarm start ringing And i woke up from this nightmare.

I wake up screaming from this nightmare. I have this nightmare everyday. But this is not just nightmare. I still live with that beast. He still rapes me whenever he want. Now i am 21 years old but I can't escape from him.

I took a deep breath and jumped into hot shower. Only hot shower can calm my anxiety. And suddenly there is a lound Bang on my door. I know who is he. The beast himself . My guardian. My only family i left.

Actually no he is not only one. I have a brother too.But he doesn't talk to me.

I came out of my deep thoughts with another bang on my door. I immediately wear a bathing robe.And I opened the door. He is in his 50s but he still look young.He is standing in front of me smrinking at me. And he see me with lust in his eyes and said- Happy Birthday Babydoll

Ughh i hate this name.

I totally forget that it's my birthday today. I said thankyou to him and he handed me a bag of louis vuitton. There is a black dress inside. He said- Wear this tonight. I want to fuck you in black. Tears pooled up in my eyes.

Atleast let me celebrate my birthday happily.- i said while sobbing.

Ohh babydoll don't cry. I'll make you happy tonight.He laughed and left me sobbing.

Chapter 2

Flashback-

Anusha baby wake up. It's time for school- My nanny said. I call my nanny- Didi. (Sister in hindi)

Ohho didi i woked up hours ago and i am ready for school. And I am big now so you don't have to come upstairs for waking me up. I can do it by myself. I said in annoying voice.

Tu chaahe kitni bhi bdii hojaa mere liye to choti hi rhegi na.. - she said with cute smile on her face. And then she left for making breakfast for me and i started keeping my books in bag.

(By the way I live in Russia and i can understand and speak hindi because of my Didi. She is taking care of me since i was born. She never talk to me in english because according to her i should know my mother tongue)

Yes yess you are getting big now. You don't need any help for getting ready to school. And I think you don't need any Nanny now. And also you are going to be 15 year old tomorrow.- He said while leaning on my room's door.

(He, My Guardian, Whom I thought of as my father, but he turn out to be beast)

His name is Zayn Khan. He is the friend of my father. He is taking care of me after my parents death. He is the same age of my father.

I wanted to call him Dad because he always take care of me like a daughter but he refused everytime. So I call him Mr. Khan.

First of all you know I don't like my birthday so please dont talk about it and secondly I always need her. She is only one who take care of me like a mother. I know you care for me too but still i need a mother figure in my life. - i said to him.

As you say baby- he said.

I smiled at him and left for school. I am sitting on window seat of my school bus. And then i saw my friend Noor's parents came to escort her to the bus.

Sometimes i really missed my parents. I didn't knew them but i Know if they were alive they do the same for me.My parents died on day when i was born. They met an accident when they are going to hospital to have me. My dad died on the spot of the accident but somehow my mother survived and paramedics took her to hospital but she also died while giving birth to me.Before my father died he said to paramedics that zayn khan will be the guardian of the baby if they don't survive. They both died on my birthday thats why I don't like it.And because of this I am living with him. I am happy with him.

What thoughts are you lost in- Noor said sitting on the side.

Nothing- i said with little smile.

Tomorrow is your birthday. What are the plans? Where are we going to the party?She asked excitedly.

Nowhere. You know noor i don't like my birthday and you also know the reason. - i said annoyingly.

Ughh Anusha it's not your fault that your parents died - she said.

I just nodded with smile.

School went same boring like always. After school i get back home and i called Didi

Didiiiii..I'm home. And I'm hungry. Give me the food- i said with hunger.

The food is on the table. - Mr. Khan said.

Where's is Didi - i askedShe is on leave for some days. She get back after some time. Go freshen up and eat your food- he said

I found this very strange because this never happend before. She never took leave without telling me. And also she was here in the morning.

But she never did this before. She always tells me when she have to take a leave.- i said.

I don't know Maybe some important work comes up so thats why - he said.

I go upstairs to freshen up and then i saw her room opend and i get inside and saw that non of her belongings is there. I get downstairs hurriedly.

Her belongings,her clothes, nothing is there in her room. Where is she? Tell me the truth- i asked angrily.

She left. I fired her from job. Because you don't need nanny at this age. It's time you should grow up and do whatever i say like a good baby- he said in masterly voice.

You shouldn't have done that. You are so bad. I hate you. And i am not eating anything untill she comes back- i said while sobbing.

Do whatever you want but she is not comming back.He said and he left me sobbing.

At night at 12pm he came to my room with small cake and said happy Birthday to me. I said thankyou and cut the cake but I'm still angry with him. And then i asked the same question to him which i am asking him on almost all of my birthdays.

Did Kabir Bhaiya called to wish me? - i asked

No babydoll. Why you don't understand that he not want to talk to you. - he said.

After that Mr.Khan go downstairs. And i go to sleep.

When i was sleeping i feel something touching me on my back and it was moving upwards. I get up quickly and i saw Mr. Khan laying behind me and rubbing his hand on my bare back. I got up quickly from the bed and turn on the light.

What the hell are you doing? Get out of my room- i said angrily.

He stood up and grab my hand and said- you are mine. I was waiting for you to grow up and become beautiful women. So i can have you in my bed. And see today you are fully grown up. - he said in his drunken voice.

My jaw dropped and tears pooled inside my eyes. I push him and ran away in the cold barefoot on the snow.

Flashback ends-

Chapter 3

Anusha POV

He close the door at my face and I am sobbing and crying continuously. But i know there is no use of this. So i just wipped my tears immediately and started getting ready for college.

I don't have any friends. I just have one friend noor whom I know since school. I am not even allowed to have a boyfriend. Mr. khan threatened me if i make a boyfriend then he will kill him. I don't want anybody to hurt because of me.

I go downstairs for going to college. And sit in the car, only his driver can drop and pick me up from college. I am allowed to do any parties, any nightovers like other girls like me. Because he own me and he don't want anyone to come near me.

I reached college and go to my class and sit beside Noor who's already excited for my birthday.

No no no… I will not listen to anything today… Today after college we are going to a party. Thoughts it.She ordered me.

Yarr..you know I can't. Mr Khan I will not let you go.- i said.

She trying to convince me again and again and i keep denying it. Finally all the classes is over and i Can go back to home. (Actually it's kind of hell for me)

I have not told any of these shit to noor. Because I am scared that he will hurt her also. She knows that something is wrong with me and she kept trying to ask me but I can't tell her.

I reached Home at 3pm afternoon. Thankfully the beast is not at home. So i go to my room and changed my clothes. I noticed the bag which he gave me in the morning and that thought is haunting me what will he do with me tonight.

At 9pm, I heard a loud bang on my door. I started shivering because i know who it is. The beastI opened the door and he was leaning on Door and he was drunk.

What did I say this morning? - he said in his drunken voice. When I come at night, you will wear that black dress. Why haven't you worn it yet?- he asked.

I was shivering badly. Its been 6 years since he was doing all this. And even today i am scared as i was the first time.

I quickly go to the bathroom with that bag and changed into that dress. And when i comeoutside he was already laying on my bed half naked.

Come. Lie down by my side - he said

I lay next to him and he immediately come on top of me. He started cupping my face with his hands and came closed to me. I can smell the alcohol in his mouth. It was disgusting and then he started bitting on my neck. Tears started coming out of my eyes. He noticed my tears and said.

By now you should have gotten used to my love- he said disgustingly

And he started doing all the bad things to me. He ripped my dress apart. Then he started pressing my breast so hard. And bitting my nipples. Then he go down on me and he took off my panties. And started fucking me with his fingers.

All these years and your cunt is still so tight- he said lustly.

I was in so much pain and crying but he didn't stop. He take out his cock and started putting it in forcefully. But it was not going inside.

Come on Babydoll, Get wet for me otherwise it will hurt more- he said.

I can't. - i whispered

Okay fine you like to do it in a painful way

He slapped me across my face. And pick up his belt and started beating me with it. I am in soo much pain and bruised right now.

Then he again take out his cock and put it inside me with force. And start thrusting fast. He rapped me again. He rapped me on my birthday.

After he was done he get up and start wearing his clothes.

Go to the bathroom and clean yourself and for fuck sake, Stop crying. It's not the first time I've done that. - he said annoyingly and go outside the room in his drunken condition.

I go to the bathroom and see myself naked in the mirror. My body is all bruised with his bitting mark and beating. I am crying so hard right now and i am in so much anger.

How long will this continue? Someday I will have to do something. I will have to tell someone. But whom should I tell who can help me? - i said to myself.

Suddenly I remember my brother. Kabir He is the only one who can help me but how? He doesn't even talk to me. And I don't have his contact number or any details. Only Mr. Khan have all his details and number but he won't give it to me.

I cleaned myself and wear clothes and get outside and i saw his phone lying on the sidetable of my bed. So I gathered all my courage to look into his phone for my brother's number.

Kabir.. Kabir where are you, where is your number? Why has he hidden the number? - i said to myself.

I have hidden it so that you cannot steal your brother's details from my phone. You cannot tell him what I do. - he said.

Panic rolled in my body. Now I don't know what will happen to me after this. I don't know whether i will survive or not.

He started unbuckle his belt.

I think I took it a little easier today... he said and starting coming near me.

'Please stay away. I will not do such a thing again'

But I will definitely get punishment for what I have done- he said

He started coming near me in his drunken state And i dont know where that courage came from but i pushed him.I pushed him so hard that he fell outside the gate of the room.And he got hit on the back of his head. Blood started running from his head.I thought it is the best chance for me to escape so i picked his phone and put it in my hoodie pocket and started running.

You can't escape from me this easily. - he hissed in pain.

He caught my leg and I fell on the ground at his side. He hold my leg and started pulling me towards him. I kicked on his face with my other leg and started running towards the stairs. He is chasing me and then he held me by my hairs. I started pushing him. And then I gathered all my power inside me and pushed him so hard that he fell on the stairs and rolled down. Then he hit his again on the floor.

Blood started pooling up near him. I started shivering. But still i go close to him and i shake him but he doesn't respond me.Then i checked his breathing.

Oh my god. He is not breathing.

Shit. Shitt. Fuckkkk - i screamed.

What have i done? I killed him. I killed him. - i started crying.

Now I don't know what will happen to me. Maybe now my life will be spent in jail. I killed him. I killed Zayn khan.

Chapter 4

Anusha POV-

My clothes were soaked in his blood. I didn't understand what to do now. I pull out his phone from my pocket and started searching his contact list in hope that someone can help me.

Suddenly i saw my Nanny (Didi) contact in his phone. I hit the call button and he picked up after 3-4 rings.

Yes Mr. Khan..everything alright... - she said and i cut her in between.

Didii.. its me Anushaa.. please come home as fast as you can.. please.. I'm in so much problem. Please come to me - i said while sobbing hardly.

Baby I'm comming in just 20 minutes- she said and cut the call.

I sat near his dead body curled up in ball and crying constantly. After 15-20 minutes later I heard a doorbell. I get up and peeked through the peephole and i saw her . My didi. I immediately opened the door and hug her like my life depends on her.

What happen baby? Why are you cryiii.. - she stopped in middle of sentence when she saw his dead body.

Oh my god. What happen? Is he alive? Let me call the ambu- lance- she said.

He's dead. I killed him. - i said

What? What are you saying? Why? - she asked

I tell her everything that had been happening to me for so many years. I tell her every detail. And I cried like a baby in her arms. She also started crying after listening to me.

Am I going to jail? - i asked her.

Nothing can ever happen to you. I am still alive, my child .- she said

She called the police. After some time lot's of police officers arrived and started asking us questions about what happened.

I tell them that he was so drunk and he slipped from the stairs. I tried helping him but I can't save him. So thats why i call the police and then call my nanny. My nanny also tell the same story to officers. Police believe our story because the crime scene looks similar to our story.

They pack his body and took him to hospital for his post-mortem and for all other formalities.

What should i do now? Where will i go now? No one left. - i started crying again because i know there's is nobody left in my family.

Don't cry baby. I am here for you.- she said and take out his phone and started searching something. Suddenly i realised his phone is still in my pocket. I took out and start searching for Kabir's contact number.

There it is . I found it. Kabir number. I finally found it.- i said with tears of happiness. But deep down i know he won't talk to me. So i give his number to didi. He knows her so i hope he can talk to her. He is my last hope to survive.

The bell started ringing.

Kabir's POV-

I was in the shower when my Phone started ringing. I don't know who is calling me at this time. I called my wife .

Shazia, honey can you pick up my phone- i said.

Yess. Wait a minute.- she said.And she start talking on the phone. I can't hear clearly but i know she is arguing with someone. I hurriedly get out of shower and wear clothes.When i came out of bathroom she was sitting on the bed sobbing.

What happen? Who is on the call? - i asked.

Who is Anusha? - she asked.

I was stunned for a minute. She kept asking me but i went completely blank. Anusha is my that secret which I never wanted to tell to shazia.

Is she your girlfriend? Or your another wife? - she asked while sobbing.

I can explain everything but let me first talk to the person who called you- i took my phone from her and dialed the last number.

Hello. Who's this? - i asked.

It's me . Anusha's Nanny. You have to come to russia right now. Mr. Zayn Khan is dead. He slipped from the stairs. And your sister is alone here. She needs you. She is not in good condition. - she said and i went completely blank again.

I am coming tomorrow- i said and cut the call.

I took a deep breath after cutting the call. Then i turned around and got down on knees in front of shazia.

Honey. Please let me explain- i said

What's left for explain? - she said while crying.

I hate Anusha. I just hate her. As soon as her name came up, my house started falling apart like it was falled 20 years ago.

She is not my wife or my girlfriend. She is my sister. Not real but step sister. My father had a slut in russia. Whenever he went to business trip in russia, he stays with her. And then she got pregnant, my mother and I didn't know any of this shit. We came to know when Zyan Khan, best friend of my father called my mother to tell that my dad had an accident and he died. And then he tells us about his whore and her daughter, my father died because he was going to hospital with that whore to have Anusha. And then my mother couldn't bear all of this. And she did suicide. Both of my parents left me alone beacause of that whore and her daughter. - I said all this with fisting my hand in anger.

And zayn Khan died today. So her nanny called me to tell me about his death. I am not cheating on you. Just give me 2 days i can go to russia tomorrow and solve all this shit. - I said.

Why didn't you keep anusha with you? Just like you she also lost both her parents. And now if there is no one else left for her, who will take care of her? She is still young. She needs somone to take care of her. - she said while wiping her tears.

I don't give a fuck what will happen to her and who's gonna take care of her. She is not my problem. I am going russia only to attend Zayn uncle's funeral. Because he was the best friend of my Dad. Nothing else. - i said angrily.

I also want to go with you. I want to meet her. - she said.

Why? Why the fuck you want to meet her. I hate her beacause of her. I lost everything. - i said.

It was not her fault. She lost as much as you lost. And i want to meet her. That's it. I am not gonna listen anything- she said stubbornly.

Fine. We're going tomorrow. Pack your bags. - i said.

And then I called Imraan, my friend to book my tickets and i tell him everything about Zayn's death. Imraan is the only one who knows about all my secrets. About Anusha.I don't know how i am gonna control my anger tomorrow after seeing her face. I saw her last time when she was just 4 year old. I hated her at just first sight. Now I don't know what will happen when i her again.

Chapter 5

K abir POV-

Next Morning we both wake up early because we are going to Russia for funeral. And also I have to think what to do with Anusha. I don't want her to be my new problem. I have enough problems already on my plate right now.That fucking Farhaad Mirza, he is my oponent in this business industry and he is also an underworld mafia boss Of Dubai. He wants to do business in Mumbai and for that first he have to deal with me. I will not let him work in my area. I will lose a lot if he succeed in his plans.But for now Anusha is my biggest problem.

We take my Private jet to go to Russia. We landed in Russia at night. It was 12pm already and our home is 2 hours away from airport.

We reached home at 2pm. I ranged the doorbell. And Nanny opened the door and welcomes us in.

The house is big, the kind in which most of the kids dreamed of growing up. Large arched windows,through them light flows through all seasons. I let my eyes wander the house. It is small than mine but yet it's beautiful.

How are you Guys? You have grown up a lot. You were just 4 years old when i first saw you. - she said with tears in her eyes and hugged Shazia and me.

You guys must be tired. Let me show you guys your room and then freshen up. I prepared food for both of you. - she said happily like a mother.

No no Didi, we already had dinner in airplane. You just show our room. We are so tired- i said while yawning.

Where is Anusha? - Shazia said.Her name only can boil my blood with anger. Why the fuck she care where is she? I don't want to lose my sleep for meeting her.

She fall asleep. She was awake for 2 night straight. She is just a child. It was so horrible for her. - she said

And i thanked God, now I don't have to see her face and ruin my sleep. She started taking us upstairs to show us our room. Funeral is tomorrow so i need sleep for that. I am so tired right now.She showed us our room and then she got downstairs for sleep.

I think this is Anusha's room - shazia said and I gave her a don't give a fuck about it look.

And then she slowly opened her door. And my eyes fell on her. She is sleeping on her bed comfortably And the light of moon fall on her face through the window. She looks so innocent and she also look just like me. And her nose look like my father's nose.

She is so beautiful. And look she have your eyes. - she said.

I left from there and get in the room. I changed my clothes and fall on bed. I didn't talk Shazia this whole time because she is just talking about how beautiful anusha is. How innocent she looks. She have my eyes and face cut..blaah blaah blaahh...And then i sleeped.

We woke up 9am in the morning and i saw shazia is not in the bed. I checked washroom and she is not here too. Then i go to the balcony and i saw She is with Anusha sitting outside with coffee and they were talking like lost best friends.And then suddenly Anusha look up to me and we have eye contact for 5 seconds. I immediately get back in my room. I felt that same anger again when i saw her first time. But it's true. Her eyes are just looked like me.

Anusha POV-

I woke up at 8am in the morning and get freshed. It was the first night in 5-6 years in which I sleep without that beast rapeing me. I am still having nightmares but i know now it's gonna be okay.

Suddenly I remember that Kabir might have arrived. His flight got late because of some issue so he tells didi that it's gonna be late.

I changed my clothes. I wore black crop top with black joggers and put my hair in messy bun and go downstairs.

Then I saw a women standing in the kitchen with didi making breakfast. And then she turned towards me and smiled.

Hey Anusha, I think you don't know me. I am Shazia Malik. Your brother's Wife.- she said hesitately and extended her hand towards me for handshake.

I shaked her hand and said Hii to her. And then i fell silent. Because I didn't understand what to say after.

She then handed me a cup of coffee and said- Let's go outside and do some chit chat. The weather is amazing here. - she said excitedly.

And then she followed me outside and we sit on small dining table in the garden.

She said how she were because of death of Mr. Zayn but it's okay. I am happy he died.

Do you know that your eyes just looked like your brother? - she asked.

I never saw him in real. But yes I saw a photo of him. But it was long ago. He must have changed now. - i said.

Suddenly I feel someone is looking at me. And my eyes go up and i saw him standing in the balcony. Shazia was saying true, he's just look like me. I tried to smile at him but he immediately go inside. I saddened by this action.

Don't worry. He'll be Okay. He just needs some time. He's not that bad- she said while my hand in hers.

I kind of liked Shazia. She is so bubbly and beautiful. Her thick short black hair, her brown eyes and red lips. She's stunning.

What are you studying And What's the plan now? - she asked suddenly

I am studying Architecture. My last year exams are starting from next month. After that I am gonna apply for job, I don't want Mr. Zayn or Kabir bhaiya's money. - i said with littlle smile.

Good. Very good. - she said proudly.

After that we go inside and get in our rooms. We have to get ready for funeral. I wore a simple black dress with long boots. Shazia goes into her room for getting ready. I was going downstairs when I saw him. Kabir, standing near sofa while texting somone on his phone. He didn't notice me or maybe he ignored me. Shazia gestured me to talk to him but i hesitate. She insisted and go to kitchen leaving me and kabir alone. I coughed. Then he looked at me and turned around. He is ignoring me.

Hey...how are you? - i asked with all my courage.

He didn't answer me. And i felt ignored and embarrassed. I give one more try.

Bhaiya... I know you don't like me but I am your sister. And I... -He cutted me off in between and turned around.

I am not your damn brother. Don't expect me that I am gonna accept you as my sister. Because of you and your whore mother, my both mother and father died. I wish you would died instead of Dad. He said angrily and stromed out of the living room.

Tears rolled down from my eyes. I didn't understand what just happened. He insulted my mother and called her whore. My tears is not stopping. Shazia was listening all this from kitchen. She came to me and hugged me tightly. And i am just crying.

I am gonna talk to him. Don't cry - she said with small tears in her eyes.

And then she wipe my tears and we go outside. Two cars were parked there. One for bhaiya and shazia and other for me and didi. Kabir bhaiya is already sitting in one car.

Didii, you go with Kabir. I am gonna go with Anusha.Shazia said and then we sit in the car.

Funeral went all went. When we went police was already there with his body. I don't want to see his face but i have to for one last time. Then People burried his body in grave yard.

May you rot in hell. - i whisper.

And then it's time to go back after all the ritual was done. Suddenly I saw two policemen are talking with kabir while looking at me. I shivered down in fear. What if police know that it was not an accident? What if they tell all this to kabir? If this happens then Kabir is going to send me in jail. Because he already hates me too much.

Shazia patted on my back and we go to the car. I was thinking about what they said to Kabir in whole car journey to home.

We reached home and I go directly to my room. I need space. Shazia came to my room and said

I know it's so hard for you. I know you can't do this alone. You need family. Come with us to India. Come to your real family and real home.

I am not believeing what is she saying.

But how? Will kabir bhaiya agree to this? - i asked.

She was saying true. I need her. I need my family. I need a new home. This house still haunts me with that old memories. But will Bhaiya agree to all this?

You just leave this thing on me. I know how to convince your brother. - she said and winks at me while leaving.

(whats police told to kabir? Did they tell him that it was not accident but murder? Did kabir gonna agree with taking Anusha to India? How's Shazia gonna convince him?)

Stay tune for know more.Please like share comment.And also tell me how's the story.Love yaa...✖

Chapter 6

Kabir POV-

She tried to talk to me while I was standing in the living room. Her voice boiled my blood in anger. I don't want to say anything to her but when she said bhaiya, I can't control my anger. I said all the mean things to her and stormed out. I know she was crying but I don't give a fuck.

I sat in the car for going to funeral and waiting for shazia but Didi sit with me instead of her.

Where is Shazia- i asked.

Ohhh she will go with Anusha in another car - she said.

Why? I don't understand at all Why shazia is caring so much about anusha? Why the fuck she care?

I said okay and curse under my breath.

We reached graveyard and I perform all my duties for his burial. I saw Shazia standing with anusha.Anusha was not sad at all, I don't why but she looks happy .

After all the ritual i said shazia to get back to the car beacause we are about to leave but suddenly one police officer want to talk to me so i go with him.

Yes officer, what do you want to talk about? - i asked curiously.

Mr. Kabir let me get straight to the point. We think that Mr. Zayn's death is not an accident. We foundy injury on his head at two places. If it was an accident than his head then there were only one injury on his head. Also Anusha called police after 45 minutes of his death. She said she was trying to save him but he was already dead at that time. We want to investigate futher but as we all know she is your sister so we investigate only if you say.

I was so fucking shocked after listening all this shit. They are saying that maybe Anusha killed him. I always knew about that bitch. She is not innocent as she looks like.

Yes, you can investigate further. I don't care if she is my sister. But if she killed him. She should be punished. - i said immediately.

They nod at me and we exchanged our number beacause i want every god damn information. and then they leave, and i also sat down in my car and started thinking what if it is true that she killed him? Why she killed him?

I reached home and directly go to my room and jumped into hot shower. I need to refresh my mind. After long hot shower i changed clothes. And suddenly a message pop up on my screen.

We have a warrent for Anusha to take her for questioning. We are coming to take her tomorrow at 11am.

I replied with okay

I put my phone down and laid on the bed. Shazia came storming to the room and started yelling on me.

What the fuck is your problem? Why you talked her so rudely in the morning? He is your brother to you Kabir. And you keep him away from yourself. This is not fair. Just like you have lost your mom and dad, he has also lost them in the same way. You should support him, he needs us, he needs the family. - she yelled.

What kind of magic has he done on you that you have started thinking that your husband is wrong? Even though he considers me his brother, I do not consider him my brother. And I will never accept him as my brother in future. And now let me sleep. This discussion ends here. - i yelled back.

I didn't know that you are like me Kabir. Why can't you see the pain in that girl's eyes? You were not that surprised Kabir. - she sobbed.

I have decided Kabir, we will take Anusha to our friend India. She needs us. She needs family.She said.

I can't control my anger. I was this close hitting shazia across her face but i stopped and stormed to Anusha's room. And i locked Shazia back in the room.

Anusha POV

I was in the shower thinking about the conversation with kabir and the officers. What are they telling him?I am scared to death right now. And also about the conversation between me and Shazia. She wants to take me India. If i go to india maybe then my life takr another turn. But will bhaiya going to agree with this?

I get out of the bathroom and getting ready to bed, suddenly I heard a lound bang on the door. At first I thought it was Zayn, maybe he is still alive but the i heard Kabir's voice.

I opend the door, he is in so much anger right now and his eyes was all red in anger. He come inside and close the door.Before i could say anything he choked me with his hands and pushed me back against the closed door.

You little bitch, what do you think you are doing? You are instigating Shazia against me, putting things in her mind that I should take you to India - he said while choking me hard. All the flashbacks are coming and I know i am having panic attack. But still i tried to speak.

Money...he did not give me any...extortion...brother, I don't want to...go...to India - i tried to speak while all choked out. Liar, you are fucking lying. What do you want? Huhh..Money, property? What the fuck do you want to stay away from us?

I don't need...anything but love..i want you to accept...me as your sister. - i said.

Never, I can't accept a murderer as my sister. I know that youu killed him, you killed Zayn but why? Because of his money or his house or property or his business , huhh tell me the fucking truth. - he said

My eyes opened wide. God he knows i killed him. But I don't want to tell him the truth.Finally he pull away his hand from my throat. I catches my breath and say-

I did not kill him. It was an accident. Why would I kill him? I don't care about his money, house, property or anything. I can kill myself.- i yelled at him.

You can tell as many lies as you want...tomorrow the police are coming to take you for questioning. Be ready for going to jail. - he said and left me alone.

I started crying heavily. My old days were better than this. I cried alot and then I saw shazia comming close to me.

Did he hurt you? What he said. I heard yelling him at you? Speak anusha - she said.

I don't want this happen to Shazia. I lied to her. And said -Bhaiya did not like that I go to India. He thought that I told this to you. It was just an misunderstanding, noting more.And Shazia I know you care for me like a sister but I don't want to come to India, maybe I'm not ready for this big change. - i lied.

Also some police officers are coming to take me, Kabir bhaiya said that they think i killed Mr. Zayn, so they want to question me. - i added.

I know this is Kabir's trick to trap you, he does not want to take you to India so he is doing all this, you have called me sister so now I will show you the sister's bank, Kabir can do whatever he wants. I know you are innocent. - she said and tucked me in bed. And she give me a hug.

Chapter 7

Anusha POV-

I didn't know when I fell asleep last night. But I woke up with loud bang on my door. I opened the door and find shazia standing with tension on her face.

What happened? Everything okay? - i asked.

There's some police officers downstairs waiting for you, they want to talk to you at police station, you have to go with them. - she said.

I totally forgot about them, Last night Kabir told me that they are gonna come. I am literally shivering in fear.

I'm ready to go, Just give me 5 minutes to get ready. - i said and she left to tell them.

I wear my clothes, I wear blue jeans with white crop top amd put my hairs in messy bun and then do downstairs, two police officers were waiting for me in the living room and Kabir is also with them. He didn't even see me walking downstairs.

I'm ready to go - i said and then they nod while standing up. They put me in the car and then we leave for station. We reached after 20 minutes. They asked me to sit in a cabin. I think it is there interrogation room. There is only one table in between and i sit on the one side. There are two chairs in front of me, and there is also a CCTV in the room.

Suddenly the door opened and two policemen come and one of them said.Let's get started, I'm Officer Richard Archer and this is Officer Casey Bree. We are the lead investigators on this case.

Okay, Ask me whatever you want. - i said.

What happened? Tell us everything in detail - Officer Casey said.

Okay, we had dinner together and then he started drinking after dinner like he always does, so i left him alone and go to my bedroom for sleeping, But I couldn't sleep, I was about to sleep when suddenly I heard a loud bang. I thought something had fallen so i called his name from my room, but there is no response, so i sleep back. After I couldn't sleep, my guts was saying something is wrong. So I get up after 10-15 minutes and started going downstairs.And suddenly I saw him poured in his old blood. I had a sudden panic attack after seeing this. But I gathered all my courage and got near him. I called his name but there is no response, I don't know what to do So i pull out his phone and called my nanny. She came after 20 minutes and then she checked his breathing and all and said that he is dead. And then we called the ambulance and police.That's all.

Why you call your nanny instead of ambulance or police? - Officer Archer asked.

Like i said I had no idea what to do. I did what I thought was right at that time. - i said immediately.

We suspect that you killed him. It was not an accident. - Officer Casey said.

Why? Why would I killed him? He was my only family. My brother doesn't like me because I am his step sister. I have no one else other than him. He was my guardian. - i said with fake tears in my eyes.

He had two scars on his head. And like you said that you only listened one lound bang. Then why there is two? - he asked.

I don't know. Maybe he get that sacr from falling on the stairs. - i said trembling.

I know why there is two scars, one from when i pushed him and his head knocked on floor. And other when he fall from stairs. I totally forgot about this. But thankfully I told everything to my nanny about what to say. Our statements have to be the same only then the police believe.

They stared me in confusion and Officer Casey saidFor now we're letting you go but you are number one on our suspect list. I know you killed him.

No I did not, It was an accident. He was the only family I left. He was like my father.- i snapped at her and wanted to puke when i called him father.

She stand silently and leave and then they let me go. I reached home after 1 hour of investigation. It was touture to me. But I have to be strong.

Shazia and Kabir was sitting in living room when i reached inside. Shazia get up and hugged me tightly. I hugged her back. Clearly Kabir is not happy that I came back. He wants me to rot in jail. I told Shazia everything they said.

This is his misunderstanding Anusha, don't worry, I will make everything right.- she said.

I just nod at her and go to my room. I need sleep, it was literally hell there.

Kabir POV

When I saw her comming, I was in so much anger. I don't want her to come back. So I got up and come to my room. And then i texted Officer Archer.

Why you let her go? - i asked.

Because we have no evidence against her. And also she have a eye witness, her nanny who also tells us the same story as her. Now we also think that it was an accident. And can't go anything without proof.

I tossed my phone on bed in anger. And then the door opened and Shazia came.

They were torturing Anusha. They were asking her if she had murdered Jain.- she said.

So, isme me kya kru? They are just doing there duty. - i snapped back.

What will you do? Will you stop them? Just tell them to close this case. It was an accident- she said.

Anusha also has to devote time to her studies. Her finals are next month. If she keeps on focusing on all this, then when will she prepare? - she added.

That's not my fucking problem.

Next day, Officer Archer called. And they said that they are going to close this case. Beacause of lack of evidence and all other proofs. It was clearly an accident. I was in so much anger because it was the only chance to get rid of her. On the other hand Shazia was happy after listening to all this. But Anusha seems normal. Like she already knew what's gonna happen. I still think she killed him.

Now we must go back to India- i said to shazia.

Yes but only with Anusha. - she said calmly.

No, she is not comming with us. - i said.

You have a problem living with Anusha, right? Fine, she will not stay with you. I will give her my old apartment. The one which belonged to my mom. She's gonna live there. Next month after completing her graduation, she's gonna come to India. She will do a job or whatever she wants to do while staying in India, she will do it.- she said.

I know that Shazia won't listen to me now. But as long as Anusha is away with me i have no problem. So i agreed. Shazia is on cloud nine right now.

We are going to leave tomorrow- i said while she is going upstairs to tell anusha all this.

I called Imraan to booked our tickets to India. And he said that Fucking Farhaad Malik are causing so much problem. He took over one of my areas. Shazia don't know about this riverly with Farhaad. But he took an oath to destroy me. Because he know I can overcome him easily. And there is another reason too. My wife Shazia.

I have to Go back to India asap. And take care of this problem. I'm gonna destroy Farhaad Malik.

Chapter 8

K abir POV

We woke up early next day. We are leaving for India today. We did our breakfast. Our luggage are already in the car. I said goodbye to Didi but I don't even look at Anusha. She tries to talk to me, saying bye to me but I ignored her. I go out and sat in the car while Shazia is still inside. She was hugging Anusha. And crying like she known her from ages. She just know her for like one week but still they are like they know each other from a very long time.

She sat in the car and we leave for airport. And we landed in Mumbai, India at night. I dropped Shazia home and go to my office beacause there is something which have to be done immediately.I called Imraan also and told him to meet me asap. Then I reached my office and sat at my chair. And then someone knocked door.

Come in. - i said.

Imraan came in with his sleepy face, and said-

This work could have been done tomorrow morning also.

No. Give me all the details. What the fuck is happened behind me? - i asked him in little anger.

Okay so when you left, Mr. Omaar Haider, the mafia king of turkey contacted us, they want some weapons from us. They are our old clients but you weren't here and this deal can't happen on call or by me. He wants you to deal with him. I tell him about death of Mr. Zayn. So he said that he is ready to wait for you to come back India,But when I called him yesterday, he said that he already got his weapons and now the deal with you guys is off. When I asked him who supplied you weapons, he said it was Farhaad Malik.He took away our old clients from us. And he has made his deal sitting in the Purple Haze Bar, which is under our area.

I clenched my teeth in anger. How he can do this? These were our rules that we would not interfere in each other's business.

We had a lot's of fight before. Many of our men where killed. To stop this bloodshed we divided our areas into two different areas and make some rules. Like he can't take away my clients and I can't take his. He will not come into my area and i will not go into his.

He broke the rules. Fix my meeting with him. - i said to imraan and he nod.

Next day I am going to meet Farhaad, I was angry all day about this.

What happen? - shazia asked.

Farhaad happend- i said.

Actually all this rivalry is from the time of my father. When my father was the biggest business tycoon of India. And he also was an Underworld Mafia and he has this enemy Farhaan Mirza, father of Farhaad, he got killed in the mutual enmity. Actually my father killed him, because he started doing human trafficking and drugs business which my father didn't like. So he killed him.Farhaad was young at that time but his uncle knows who killed his brother, and they killed my dad in revenge when he was in russia with that whore and having his daughter. Everybody knows that it was an accident but It was Farhaad's Uncle behind it. He tried to kill us too but we escaped because of Mr. Zayn. And after when I took over my Dad's business. Farhaad did the same and become my enemy. This is our generational enmity. Farhaad wants to take me down and want to become the King of India, he took an oath to destroy me, so he keeps playing his little games.

What has he done now? - she asked curiously.

He took away my clients from me while I was in russia solving all this shit because of that bitch---

Don't talk about anusha like that, she is your sister- she cutted me middle.

Why the fuck you care about her so much? - i asked.

Because I feel her love for you. For us, Her nanny told me how she always asking about you in her childhood and now. She always wanted to live with you. She always wants her brother to be her side. I saw her love for you, for us.. in her eyes. - she said

I don't give a fuck about her love - I said and stormed out of house and leave for the meeting.

Farhaad POV

That motherfucker Kabir wants to meet me. And I know why. But the matter is simple. First come first serve. I am sitting in my black aston martin going to meet that motherfucker.

I reached his office and asked receptionist about him and she tell me the way drooling her eyes all over me. I don't like these kind of bitches.

I reached in his office and knocked the door.

Yes , come in - he said.

I go inside and sit on chair in front of him. He was already in anger or maybe he's look like this. I don't know what her wife likes in him.

Let me get straight to the point, you broke the rules. It was my fucking deal which you took away from me. How dare you did that? - he said while clenching his teeth.

Because you were not here. And he needs weapons urgently. So I supplied him, simple - i said carelessly.

He was ready to wait for me to come back. You knew I was not in the country so you called him. You did that on purpose, and now you have to pay back to me. - he said.

I laughed like a devil. He wants my money. Fuck him, I am not giving him a single penny.

I got up and said - No, I'm not gonna give you anything. Do whatever the fuck you want.

Oh I will. You just wait and watch - he said while challenging me. And I started leaving giving him a smrink.

BTW, where were you? - he said.

That's none of your fucking business - i replied with anger.

Ohh okay, I thought you were in Russia, you know there was going to be a huge arms deal. But nevermind I got the deal. - I winked at him and leave

I thought that arms deal was the biggest deal for kabir, he was planning for it from a long time. But he didn't show up. So the deal directly goes to me. I don't know what's important than that for him. But who cares, I got the deal and I was so happy seeing his face red in anger.

Chapter 9

Its been a week since Kabir and Shazia go back to India. And today I'm going to my college again after all this shit happened in my life. I don't have any friends in college beacause of zayn i have so many trust issues that I don't believe anyone. I totally lost my faith in friends and love shit.

I wear a full sleeve pink crop top with blue denim jeans. My nanny is still with me untill my exams are over and I goes to India. My exams are in 15 days and I have to cover alot. Shazia still calls me everyday and we talked alot. Actually she is my only friend i have. But I have noor also. (Remember...my school friend)She is still with me but she doesn't know any shit and I also not gonna say anything to her. I text her that I am coming to college today. She replied excitedly. Then I head out and reached college.

Heyyyyy...how are youuu?? I heard about Mr. Zayn passing. I'm so sorry. - she said.

Thankyouu Noor. And I'm totally fine now. - i replied.

So what are you gonna do next? You don't even have any family left - she asked sadly.

Actually I have a family. - i said happily.

What? Who? Do you have a boyfriend or something? Why didn't you tell me about? I want to meet him?

She asked me loads of questions in just one breath.

No no, I don't have any boyfriend. But I have a brother. Remember I told you about Kabir. He and his wife Shazia came here for the funeral. Kabir is still upset and angry with me but his wife shazia, she's so supportive and caring. And she wants me to come to India after graduation. - i said.

Whattttt? Indiaa?? No, way you are not going to leave me alone here. What about our plans? Our dream jobs? - she asked sadly.

I know but I have to go to India. There is no one here for me. And I can do any job there. - i said.

Okay fine. But don't forget about me. - she said.

I'm not going tomorrow. Don't act senty. I still have one month left. - i said.

Okay fine. - she said and hugged me. Then we go to our classroom and after classes she helped me with all the pending stuff. I get home at 7 in the evening and I just got freshed and starting studying for my exams.

After 1 month

Today all my exams are over. Today I'm tension free from all the things. Shazia called in the morning that she is coming to get me on my graduation day which is after one week so I have to start packing all my stuff now and I called noor to help me. She is coming in the evening and we also having girls sleepover.

I think it's first time in my life that I am living all the big small moments. Zayn would never let me do all this. Now I am happy that he died.

Someone knocked on my door. It is noor.

Hey gurllll.. how are you? - she asked.

Sexy as always.. - i replied laughing.

Ohh yess.. you are sexy. But what to do with this sexy, when it's no fun like parties boyfriend and sexxx - she said i made annoyed face.

We are having fun tonight on our girls sleepover. - i said.

Uffff... I'm not talking about this fun. Come on naa..let's go to club. Let's have party. Anyway you are going to leave after week. So let's enjoy naaa..pleasee - she said with her puppy eyes.

I also think that I want to have fun too. And there is no Zayn here to stop me. I also have to lived my life to fullest. So I said yes. And she jumped in excitement.

But we can't go there like this. I'll have to get you a dress.- she gestured at me with her hand. She go back home. And came back with lots of dresses. And chose black mini dress which looks least sluttery among all of them.

At 9pm we started getting ready do Noor do my makeup. I saw myself in the mirror, I looked beautiful. Really beautiful and little hot and sexy.And I put my hairs in bun and add some silver jewellery with black heels.

We reached Propaganda Night club one of the biggest club in Moscow, Russia. Interior is so good and dark. Music was beating in my ears. It was so loud. It's my first time coming to any club. I was feeling very strange.

Lets drinkkkkkk - Noor yelled.

I never drink before. - i replied hesitatly.

There is first time for everything - she said and dragged to me the bar counter and ordered vodka shots.

I drank in one breath and feel burning sensation in my throat. But It goes away after 2 more shots. And then she dragged me to the dance floor. We dancend for alleast half and hour. And came to the counter after we got tired. My heels are bitting my legs.

I never had this much fun in my entire life. - i said to noor. Me tooo - she replied.

Suddenly waiter gave us two drinks. And we told him that we don't ordered this. And he gestured to his right side and that they ordered for you. There were two boys sitting holding glasses in hands and one of them wave at me. We denied there drinks and get back to our chitchat and we drink alot. I started feeling dizzy and I need to use the washroom. Noor was dancing his ass off on the floor so I don't disturb her and go to the bathroom alone.Bathroom was empty and that is good for me. I washed my hands and cleaned my mouth. I am feeling soo dizzy right now that I can't stand by myself.

Suddenly someone closed my mouth with his hands from behind. I didn't realize what happened at all and the he speaks -How dare you to say no to me? Maybe you don't know about me. Let me show you who I am.

Suddenly all my memories of getting raped are getting back. All my nightmares are dancing in my eyes again. Tears started comming from my eyes. I kept trying to push him. But he was so strong I can't do anything. He was stronger than Zayn. I am having panic attack from all this. He started opening my dress from behind and started kissing on my neck. All the bad memories are coming one by one again. Maybe this is just my life.

But then I feel someone pulled him. I took deep breaths and turned back after few seconds, I saw someone hitting him on his face. I can't see his his face because his back was towards me. My eyes are getting closed because of alcohol or my panic attack.But i still stand up and run towards the door without seeing what is happening behid me. I just run run and run towards noor, I dragged her from the dance floor towards the exit and we sit in Noor's car and got away.

When we reached home, i felt a sigh of relief.

What happened anusha? Why you dragged me here? We were having so much fun. - she said.

I told her everything what happened in the bathroom and how a stranger saved me .

Oh my god, I'm so sorry. Are you okay? - she asked.

Yes I'm fine. Lets just sleep. I still feel dizzy - i said.

And then we changed clothes and sleeped. I still having thoughts about that stranger who saved me. I don't even say thank you to him. Who knows who it will be?

Chapter 10

Farhaad POV

I was in my private jet going Russia for Arms deal. To destroy Kabir, first I have to take all this clients from him. So that he has nothing left. I took a sip from my glass of champagne and looked over my airhostess, she is already looking at me with her seducing expression.Actually I can have a little fun here. So I grabbed her and made her sit on her knees.I unbuckled my pants and gestured her to take over.She grabbed my already hardened dick and took it in her mouth. She gave me a blowjob for 15 minutes.

She her is mouth is full of my dick and tears are running down from her eyes ruining her makeup. After that she was started gagging and having difficulty in breathing and then i cummed into her mouth and she swallowed all my cum like a slut.

Then I threw her away and goes to bathroom to clean myself. Bitches like her are only for use and throw.

I landed Russia in the evening and go to my hotel.And a message popped up from the clients. It was the location of Propoganda night club, it was the biggest night club in russia, I've been there before.

After reaching to my hotel room, I took a long shower, had my dinner and took a short nap.After waking up I started getting ready for the club.I wore a black shirt with black pants and white shoes, get into my car and leave for the location.

I reached the club and go to the VVIP room there and I saw my client sitting there. That meeting went on for 2 hours. Now he didn't do deals with Kabir, but from me. I was very tired after the meeting, so I go to the Bar counter and ordered whiskey. And eye fall on the dance floor. I saw her.My eyes just stuck on her.She is the most beautiful girl I ever saw. She looks like an Angel.My Angel.She was dancing, like peacock dances in rain, like butterfly fluttering in the air. So beautiful.

Suddenly she disappeared, I started looking for her, she is going to the bathroom, I followed her through the crowd.When I entered the bathroom to see her, A man was grabbing her from behind and he tries to rip her dress. My blood started boiling in anger.

I grabbed him from behind and pull away from her. She closed her eyes and sat down to catch her breath. I know she is having panic attack, I was going to help her but he attacked me from behind and I turned to him and started punching on his face. When I again turned to look at her, she disappeared, I looked at the door and it was fucking open, she ran. I tried to run to her but that motherfucker grabbed my leg and started pulling me, I took the gun out of my pocket and shoot him from point blank.

Nobody touches my Angel. She is mine. - i said to his dead body.

I ran outside but she is nowhere to be seen. I searched the whole club, every fucking corner for about half and hour but she is not there. My angel runs away beacause of that fucker.

Suddenly a man came in black suit to me, he looks like he's an bouncer here. Mr. Wilston wants to see you. - he said.

Max Wilston, owner of the Propaganda Night club and old friend of mine. He 24 years old and open this club on his own, we met in college and after that he became my friend. He deals with all the matters happen in Russia for me, This Kabir deal is also cracked by him for me.

That bouncer opened the door for me and i entered into his cabin.

There's a fucking dead body in the bathroom of my club, CCTV shows that you were inside before my cleaner founds the body and infroms me. Why the fuck you do that? - he asked.

This is easy for you to clean this shit. There is no need to called me here. - i said.

It is easy, I already get rid of his body and CCTV footages but why the hell you killed him? - he asked again.

He tries to touch her. When I opened the door of the bathroom, he was fucking grabbing her. My blood boiled in anger, I tried to stop him, but he didn't stop. He invited his own death - i said while grinding my teeth.

Who was she that you are so crazy about? I never seen you before like this. You use and throw womens and today you killed the person who touches her? What happened to you? - he asked.

I don't know who was she? But I'm gonna find her- i said while smirking.

You don't know her and you killed the person who touches her. - He claps his hand while saying this.

I want to see the footages. I want to know who was she and where she gone. - i said.

Fine, come here. - he said and I started seeing all the footage very closely. And then I saw her. No matter how much I looked, but my eyes are not getting satisfied. I want her. I want to touch her. Her face. Her hair. Everything.I'm gonna make her mine.

Max was right, what the fuck is happened to me. She's just ordinary girl. Why I am feeling so obsessed with her? This never happens before, I don't know what will happen next? I need to find her.

I asked Max to find her for me, he knows every corner of Moscow, he will find her for me.

I called Jibraan.

Jibraan is my other best friend and also my Right hand. I told him about my Angel and other details of the deal. He was also shocked like Max, but the truth is I was also shocked. She didn't even look at me but still she did some kind of magic on me. That's why I named her Angel.

I got back to India next day beacause I can't leave my business but Max assure me that he will find her.

It's been one week here. Max couldn't find her. I was so pissed at him that he can't find a girl. But he said he will try his best and next day he come to my office in India, I was shocked to see her. I was about to ask why he's here but suddenly he slammed the file on my table. I opened the file and pulled out a photograph, the photo is of my Angel. And this file contains all the details of her.

You can send me this file via WhatsApp, pdf or any way. Why did you come to India for this? - I asked.

Max was looking so terrified. Suddenly Jibraan also came to my cabin, he also looks the same as Max.

What the fuck happened to your faces? - I asked them both.

Actually I checked the CCTV footage of the parking lot, hopefully to find the vechile in which she came to the club, and I find it.

I immediately check the number plate and found an address of some girl, Noor. I thought she was Noor, and it was her car but when I looked deep inside, she was not Noor, So I gathered all the information on this girl Noor like her friends, her college etc.While checking Noor's social media, I found your girl.Her name is AnushaAnusha Malik. - Max said and I am feeling so good that he do all this to me.

Thankyou so much max, I'll come to Russia and now I can handle all this myself- I said and Jibraan interrupt me.

You don't have to go to Russia, She completed her graduation and she is coming to India for setting here.That night in the club, Noor was giving her farewell party. - Jibraan said.

I was on clound Nine after listening to this. I said thankyou to both of them, I am literally obsessing over her. I want to see her again. Meet her, I want to listen her voice. And Fuckk yess It was early but I want to kiss her juicy lips so badly.

From the last week, she is the only one running inside my mind. I want her and only her. She's mine to touch, Mine to kiss , Mine to fuck.

You have to listen all the details before saying thankyou, we are terrified beacause what I'm going to tell you now, you are gonna be so pissed. - Max said.

Just tell me - i said.

She's Kabir's sister. Kabir hide her from all of the world, he never bring her to India, that's why we don't know, Kabir had kept her in Russia with his father's friend. Zayn.Remember when Kabir was not here, we took his deal from his hand, he was in Russia with Anusha, actually Zayn died. So now there is no one in Russia who can take care of Anusha, so he decided to bring her to India. And she came yesterday.Jibran said.

Get out of my office right now.- i yelled at both of them. And they get up and head out.

When I first saw her, I thought that maybe I fall in love with her. But It turned out that the girl I fall in love is my Biggest enemy's sister. How can I love her.All the love for her turned out to be in anger. But now I have a plan to destroy to kabir.

Chapter 11

Anusha POV-

It's been 1 week since the incident of the club happened. I'm still wondering about that stranger who helped me. Also I'm still sacred that what will happen if he come back?

Leave it. - i said to myself.

Tomorrow I'm going to India, my packing is already done with the help of Didi and Noor. They are so emotional right now because I'm leaving tomorrow.I'm so nervous right now that what will happen? Shazia said that she will pick me from the airport in India and then we head to home. I spent the whole night thinking about how things will be there?

Next day morning-

I'm checking all the documents which will I need in the airport, and I rechecked everything and now I'm all set to go.

I say my final goodbyes to Noor and Didi, they both cried alot, But I tell them that we get in touch through phones. Then I leaves for the airport.I reached airport in the morning and boarded my flight, It was whole new experience for me, travelling alone and all. I landed in India at night and came outside the airport searching Shazia.

Anushaaa - Shazia yelled and tightly hugs me. How was the journey? How are you? - she started throwing questions.

I'm fine and journey was also good. - I said.

Her driver puts all my luggage in the car and we sat together in the backseat of her Mercedes Maybach.

Anusha, I want to talk to you about something- she said and I nod.

Actually I convinced Kabir to bring you here but he is not ready to keep you in our house. - She said.

So, Where will I stay? - I asked.

In my home. Actually my old apartment, where I live before marriage. Its just 15 minutes away from our house. So you can stay there and If you have any problems or anything in future, I am gonna just 15 minutes away from you. - She said.

I feel so overwhelmed from her. She is just taking care of me like any mother did to her child. But she still feel guilty that she could not convince Kabir about me living together with them. But still she did a lot for me. And I know one day Kabir will do the same when he understands how much I love him as my big brother.

But for now we are going to our house. You are going to your new apartment tomorrow- She said.

But what about Kabir? - I asked.

Umm.. he knows that you are coming. I handeled him already- she said and winks at me and I smilied.

We reached home after half and hour. And my jaw dropped when I saw the house. It was so beautiful and perfect, like we see in the movies. White and black from outside with garden and pool. It was just amazing.

We head inside and the interior was amazing like if we had any word other than amazing that would be it.

Her househelpers took my luggage upstairs.Anusha go upstairs with them and freshen up and come downstairs for dinner, Kabir is also going to join us.- she said And I started following them.He showed me my room and left. Room is also fabulous as the whole house. And the room is also white with the shades of brown and when I pulled back the curtain there is mesmerising view of the beach. And it was just breathtaking.

I go to the bathroom and took long hot shower and get outside and wear my night pjs with crop top. And ready to go downstairs. I don't know how Kabir's gonna react after seeing me.

Kabir POV-

I reached home after long tiring day and entered the house. I saw shazia standing in the kitchen with bowls and she was getting the table ready for the dinner.

What's the matter? So much preparation for what? - I asked while hugging her from behind.

Heyy... Did you forget? Anusha has come today. I just brought her here from the airport, she's upstairs freshning up. - She said and my blood boiled.

I told you not to bring her here. I don't want that bitch in my house. I -- I stopped talking and saw her, she was standing little far from us while listening all this.

I'm sorry. I'll come later.- she said and started leaving but shazia stopped her.

No anusha. Go sit on the dinning table. We are going to have dinner together.- Shazia said.

I am leaving- I said and go outside from the house and sit in the car and leave. I know shazia calling me from back but I don't listen to her and just get away. I can't live with him for even one night.I go to Imraan's place and told him about everything that happened and he said let's to our club and chill.

We reache Illusions club, In this club all the mafia's and underworld people came for meetings and get some fun. We reached and sit on the table.

So what will you do you? She's here. - Imraan asked.

I don't know but I can't live with her. Shazia said that she will give old apartment of hers to anusha. But she will be just 15 minutes away from me. I don't know what to do with that bitch.

Maybe you should give her a chance. Maybe you should talk about the differences you have with her. No matter what, but she is your sister. - he said.

You are also talking like Shazia, and she is not my sister, tomorrow any daughter of whore said that she is my sister, so Im gonna accept that? No fucking way, she is not my sister. She's just the daughter of the whore which my dad fucked. - I said in anger.

So what will you do? Kill her or what? - he asked.

Maybe. I will kill her. - i said and finished my drink.

Anusha POV

Shazia was so upset with the behaviour of Kabir. He just left us there. He didn't even look back to us. We did our dinner without Kabir, I thought that I will talk to him on the dining table, if he's not talking then I will take the first step but he leaves. I feel so sad about shazia and I consold her.But deep down I know that it's because of me, I came here and fucked their lovely relationship.

I know it's because of me. You shouldn't have brought me here. - I said.

No its okay. You had to come sometime. And I know his heart will definitely melt. - she smiled .

After dinner we had some chit chat and she tell me all about mumbai, tomorrow we are going to her house and she's gonna help me to settle. And after that we are going for shopping and she's gonna show me mumbai. I am excited for this new journey of mine.

(what's new challenges anusha going to face in her new journey? Will Kabir's heart melt or is he gonna same forever? Did kabir really want to kill anusha?)

Stay tune to know more. Vote share comment.Thankyou.Love yaaa...✖

Jo log bhi story padh rhe hai..please tell me in the comments how story is? And please no hate comments, It's my first time writing. Please tell me in the comments.✖

Chapter 12

Anusha POV-

I woke up with the sunlight touching my face. It was only 9am. I go in the garden downstairs, and feeling the cold wind on my body. I was standing with my eyes closed and breathing the fresh air. Suddenly I feel somone is behind me, I turned back and saw Kabir standing, maybe he just arrived home because he's still in his office clothes from yesterday.

Why are you here? - He asked.

Because you are my family. - I replied.

Bullshit..just tell me the truth what the fuck you want? - He asked again.

I told you. I don't want anything. I can earn myself. - I said proudly.

He made his angry face and started going inside.

Just give me a chance. I also lost both of my parents like you. I've never even seen them in real life. Atleast you know how dad was. I don't know anything. I only seen one photo of dad, and I couldn't even find one photo of my mother. At least you know about what parent's love and care feel like. (My tears are flooding from my eyes)

And you want to know why I'm here? Just for your love and care, nothing more. I don't want anything. I'm here because I want someone I can call family-I said with tears flowing from my eyes, I don't know why I'm so hurt right now, I just ran from there.

I ran upstairs to my room opening the door so hard. I curled into ball and cry my heart out untill my eyes become sore, why me? Why the hell this is all happening to me? Will I ever find love? Will there be someone who will love me? And then I didn't realise when I fell asleep.

Kabir POV-

I seriously want to kill her. Why she is here? I know she's here just for money. I can throw any amount of money she said but just go away from here.All these thoughts are coming up while I was driving back home, I spent my night at Imraan's place. I didn't feel like going home but I have to, for changing my clothes and also for apologising to Shazia, I was soo rude to her last night. And deep down I was praying that I don't want tosee her when I was reached home.

I parked my car in parking area and when I was entering the door I saw her standing in the garden. She was inhaling deep breath of cold air, warm sunlight falling on her face, my legs started moving towards her, When I see her closely, she looks just like Dad, her eyes are like him, suddenly She feels that I was standing behind her. She opened her eyes and turned around.

I don't know why I am here, I was praying not to see her just 5 minutes ago. My anger came back and threw a question towards her.I was turning after our heated conversation but I stopped when I listened to her, she didn't even see her mother's face? How? Why? Mr. Zayn should have shown her a photo of her mother. My heart ached after listening to her, after saw her crying.Why my heart is fucking melting? I don't want this. I wanted to leave but before I go she went away crying. I feel so bad that I made her crying. Why the fuck I'm feeling this way.

After that I went inside and apologised to shazia, I know she's still upset but I do this right.I'm still feeling strange about what happened to me in the garden, I feel bad for her? Why? I was questioning myself. I have to go to upstairs for something. And when I saw her lying on the floor, I get nervoused first, I thought something happened to her, I ran towards her and check her. I heard a little snort sound and realised that she was just sleeping. And I took a sigh of relief.

She fell asleep while crying, I can see her dry teards on her cheeks. I wiped her tears with my fingers,(why the fuck I did that? Is my heart melting?) And then I picked her up in my arms and put her to bed. And covered her with the blanket.

Why? Why the fuck I am here? Why I'm doing this? I should not be here. I hate her. I fucking hate her. She stole my everything from me.- I whispered in anger to myself and stromed out of the room.

Anusha POV

I wake up with the bang on my door. I opened my eyes and check my phone, It was 12noon.

Shit!!!why the hell I slept this long? - I asked to myself and get out of the bed hurriedly and opened the door. It was shazia on the door.

Hey Sleeping beauty.. I hope I'm not disturbing you.She said jokingly.

Sorry, I slept this late. I waa having trouble in sleeping last night, you know it's new place.- I lied.

Hehehe..it's okay anusha. You skipped breakfast so now are going to have lunch outside. And after lunch I'm going to show you your new house. So go fast and get ready, I'm waiting for you.- she said and I nod. Then she go downstairs. And I closed the door.

While I turned around,all the memories from morning flooding in my mind. Meeting Kabir in the garden, crying in front of him, crying in the room and sleeped on the floor.Waittt!!!! I sleeped on the floor. I know, I remember I sleeped on the floor. Who put me to the bed?Is it Kabir? If not kabir then who?

Chapter 13

Anusha POV-

I take shower and get ready. I wore a simple blue straight denim jeans with dark pink shirt and my OG white shoes. I like wearing loose clothes.

I dont wear clothes which shows too much skin. Like I want to wear but they are still marks on my body given by that beast, Zayn.

I go downstairs and Shazia was already waiting for me. I'm sorry to keep you waiting. - I said.

It's okay Onuu. - she said while pulling my cheeks. I feel so loved by this gesture of hers. She really take care of me like a mother.

We got into our car. The same Mercedes Maybach, I loved that car.

First, we are going to have lunch and then I show you your apartment. And also we are going to my favourite restaurant. - she said.

Okay. I'm excited to see India and of course my new home. - I said.

I spent the entire journey looking out from the window. I saw soo many stalls and shops and so many people on road. Tall buildings, big malls and of course, the beautiful- Mumbai Sea Link.

We reached after half an hour drive. The restaurant was so big and amazing. The Celestial.

We eat our lunch and talked alot. Talking to her feels so good. I enjoyed our girls time alot. I forgot all my problems with her. After lunch we are going to my new home. We reached and I saw a huge building in front of me. We parked our car in the underground parking lot and take elevator to go upstairs.

The apartment is on the 15th floor. And you can see the amazing view of Mumbai sea link from and the balcony and beautiful sunsets and sunrise. - She said. I got more excited after listening all this. We reached on our floor. And there is only one more apartment on that floor besides mine. We got out of the elevator and she pull out the keys from the bag and opened the door. And my jaw dropped. It was so fucking beautiful. When we enter from the door, there is a living room. It's in the shade of black and white, it feels so cozy. The apartment is not that big it was so beautiful. I always want that type of house. There is a couch with huge tv and the dining table. And there is a balcony also. And huge chandelier. Beautiful.

Let me show you the house. - she said and we turn to right. In the right there is a small kitchen with same black and white pattern.

And to the left there are two rooms. Take any of the room which you like. - she said and opened the first room.

It was so simple yet elegant. The interior was so good. I'm also an architect. And I gave 10 out of 10 to this house. And the she showed me second room.

I'll take the second one. - I immediately said. It has attached walking wardrobe. And it looks so elegant. The whole is so perfect. Then I saw the walking wardrobe from inside. It was fricking beautiful. And in front of it there was a bathroom.

There's still some clothes of me and your brother in the closet. Today I can settle all this. - Shazia said.

I go to see the bathroom walking through the closet.It was beautiful too.

After seeing all the house. We came back to living room and sat on the couch.

So Did you like the house? - She asked.

Like?? I love it. I always wanted this type of home. Small yet cozy. Thankyouu so much for all this. I can move out to my place as soon as I find the job. - I said.

You don't have to say Thankyouu and don't move out. This place is now yours. You know Kabir had bought this house for me before we got married. After that I shift to his place and since this house was closed. I always wanted that someone can live here. There are lot of memories of me and Kabir here. - she said and got emotional.

I'll take of this place like you did. - I said while holding her hand.

Suddenly Door bell rang, Shazia opened the door and there's a lady in Saree come inside.

Anusha...meet Priya, your house help. She can clean cook and do everything for you. She will come from tomorrow and also she doesn't know how to speak english so you have to talk to her in hindi. - she said.

It's okay. I know how to speak hindi. Didi taught me well. - I said and say hii to priya.

Then Shazia explained the whole house work to her and then she leaves. Come on let's go home now. - She said.

I wanted to live here from today. - I said.

But Anusha, you can come tomorrow with all your stuff. - she said.

No, please can you send all my stuff today? I want to live here and also I don't want that kabir fight with you again today because of me. - I said in pleading way.

She says ok and then she leaves after goodbye hug. I opened the balcony and see a beautiful view of sea link and I took out my phone to take the picture but there is one obstacle, there's a huge building on the left side which ruined my photo. There is a huge name plate attached on the top floor of the building. I think it's some kind of office on the bottom floors and the top is penthouse. If this building was not here then the view would have been more better. The name plate reads - Mirza's

I got inside and someone rang the bell. I opened the door, there is a girl standing in front of me with huge smile on her face. She's same age as me.

Hello. My name is Alana Sharma. - She said while and extended her hand for handshake.

I shaked her hand.

I'm Anusha Malik. - I said.

I think you just shift here. I saw you two comming from the balcony. I live in this side apartment of yours. - She said.

I invited her inside and we both sat on the couch.

Yes. I just shift here today. Actually it's my sister-in-law's apartment. - i said.

Ohh I see. - she said and her phone rang and then she stood up and I stand up with her.

Look If you need anything. You can come to me. I'm here for you. I know Shazia. She lives here before you. She is my friend, so you are my friend too. Just knock on my door anytime. And yes if you want to explore Mumbai, we can do this together.- she said and jumped with excitement.

I like her. So kind and bubbly.

Of course we can explore together. I'm new here and need a friend too. - I said while smiling.

Okay fine. Let's go clubbing tonight. You okay with this? - she asked.

No. I don't want to go to clubs. - I said because all th memories from the club of russia are getting back. I don't to put myself into that position again.

Why? - she asked with sad face. I don't like places with so much noise. I like quiet places. Do you have something in you mind? - I asked.

There's a cafe just 5 minutes away. And in that cafe there is a library too. We can go there. - she said.

Perfect- I replied.

So get ready till 5pm in the evening. We are going there. - She said leaves jumping in excitement.

I'm so happy here. I felt nervous before coming here. But now I feels that everything is going to be Okay. With shazia and ofcourse with my new friend Alana.I'm excited now for this journey.

Chapter 14

A nusha POV -

I don't know whether my life will be on track by staying here or not. But I am hoping my best for me. I started getting ready in the evening because Alana and I going to a library cafe at 5pm. Shazia send all my luggages to my new home and calls me to ask for any help. I said no to her and I also tell her about Alana, she said that Alana is good friend So I can also make her my friend.

I wore black crop top with black baggy jeans and white shirt on top of crop top and left my hair open, and wore my OG white sneakers and got ready.

My door bell rang at sharp 5pm. I opened the door, Alana standing in front of me wearing brown dress. She looks pretty.

Are you ready to go? - she asked.

All set!!! - I replied.

We will go there on foot because It will take only 10 minutes walk to reach there, if we take any any vechicle, we could get stuck in traffic. - She said.

Okay. No problem. - I said

I grab my purse and locked the house and then we go downstairs by elevator. And after 10-12 minutes of walk we reached there. The cafe was looking fabulous from outside. It was giving the vintage vibe. There was a very nice smell of coffee coming from inside.

So Did you like it or not? - she asked.

I love it!!! - I replied.

The Cafe was so beautiful from inside too. There are less people in there which I loved. We sat on the table and waiter comes for the order. We ordered our coffees and waiter show us the different types of book to read. We choose our books and started reading and talking to each other.

So how do you feel coming to India? - she asked.

India is good. I like it here with my family. Kabir and Shazia. - I said.

And what was Russia like? - She asked.

Russia was also good. You know, There were family too. But to be honest I like here more. - I replied with smile.

So what's your next plan now? - She asked.

I want to open this type of cafe. It was my childhood dream. But for now, I need a job. I am an architect with no experience. I can do interviews design, I can make a whole map of any building or house. I.Can.Make.Everything. But who will give me a job without experience and also without internship. - I asked all this in just one breath with my sad face.

Umm..Actually I can help you with that. I have a friend who is opening his new studio. He needs a interior designer. And I think you are perfect for that. I can talk to him. - She said.

Thats so sweet of you. But do you think that I can do that? - I asked with nervousness.

Ofcourse you can. Just give me your number. I give that to him and he will give you all the details. Then you decide that you can do it or not. By the way he's Photographer, so he needs his office like that studio for photography. - She said.

Okay I will give it a try. And thankyou so much. - i said.

Ohho..shut up yar.. we're friends. No sorry, No Thankyouu. - she said and both of us laughed.

After that we talked more about our past lifes and she tell me about her past relationships and her past life. We talked about all girl's stuff. It was amazing having a friend like her. We sat for almost 2 hours in that cafe. It was already dark outside and we left from the cafe and started walking to home.

It was beautiful night. And the time I spend with her was also beautiful. When we reached near home, the building that was visible from my window came to view.

Whose building is this? This building has ruined my view of Sea Link. - I said while laughing but her face turned dark.

What happened? - I asked again.

This building belongs to the Devil himself. Just don't look at that building. He is the most ruthless and biggest Mafia boss of underworld. Everybody in this country scares of him. Even any government officials or police cannot do anything. He also have business in other countries.- She said with scary face.

Oh ok. But why should we be afraid? We didn't done anything wrong to him. - I said.

Yeah but still.. his building itself scares me. Imagine what would he be like. - She said. And I just nod twice.

We get back to our building and said bye to each other. After I reached home I took a cold shower because there were lots of humidity outside. And then I changed into my pjs. It was almost 9pm and I am hungry now. There is all the ingredients available in the kitchen but I don't feel like cooking. I took out my phone and ordered pizza. It arrived after 30 minutes.And then I sat in the balcony with pizza and my laptop. My eyes are stuck on that building. I was so curious and wanted to know Who is that Devil Alana talking about.I opened google on my laptop and started searching him. I wrote Mirza and Co. in the search bar. And there is all the information showing about it. I started looking at that information closely.He is not only business but he also deals in Arms, He sells arms to other countries and also human trafficking, drugs and what not.

Then I searched the owner of this company. His name and photo shows up.He name is Farhaad Mirza. (Devil)I clicked on the photo, he is most handsome and sexiest man I ever saw. Long black wavy hair, deep and dark black eyes, he was wearing black and white suit in every photo. He really look like the The Devil himself.

I was looking into more about his enemies and other stuff but my phone rang. It was Shazia.

She asked me about my day. I tell her everything about me and Alana goes to cafe and how she offered me a job at her boyfriend's place. Shazia was so happy about my first job. Then she cut the call because Kabir arrived. I shut my laptop and go inside. And my phone rang again. It was an unknown number. I picked up and Alana's friend Aahaan is on the other side of the phone. We talked about everything about the project and now I think I can do this. He wants me to see the place and start working on it asap. I am going tomorrow with Alana to see the place. I was so happy. My life is finally come on track. It would be better if it doesn't get messed up now.

Chapter 15

Anusha POV-

Last night I didn't even realise when I fell asleep, I woke up because of the warm sunlight was falling on my face. I sat on the bed with a limp, suddenly I realise that I had to meet Ahaan, Alana's friend for my new job. I literally run towards bathroom and got freshen up and took shower and run towards wardrobe for clothes. I didn't know what to wear. I thought I should wear something formal for wear.

I wore light beige formal pants with black top tucked inside. Put my hairs down and my sneakers. I look good in that.

When I got ready, I got call from Alana. She was asking me If I was ready for today. And told me to meet downstairs.

I picked up my black bag and locked my house and go downstairs in hurry. I saw Alana standing beside her car.

Heyy..you look fab..but you're late. - Alana said.

I know, I know. I'm soo sorry. I didn't realise when I fell asleep last night. I forgot to set the alarm. - I said.

It's okay anusha..let's go. - She said.

We both sat in the car and it was 1 hour long drive with heavy traffic. I almost fall asleep in the car out of boredom.

We are about to reach our destination. - Alana said.

I got up and sit straight and take out comb out of my bag and redoo my hair. Alana parked the car and We both get out.

Ahaan said that his studio is on the 18th floor. - Alana said and I just nod.

We reached upstairs by the elevator and there is a door across the hall, we knocked the door.

And A handsome man opened the door and gave smile to both of us.

Anusha, this is Ahaan and Ahaan , this is Anusha- alana introduced us.

Ahaan was, well different. Yes, different. He was handsome not perhaps in the conventional sense but he had that appearance which could make him stand out in the crowd. He was fair, godlen brown eyes, black-brownish hairs. He was handsome.

Heyy Anusha. It's so nice to see you finally. - He said.

Same here Ahaan. - I said.

So let's get to work. - he said.

Umm.. actually i have some work pending, so I'm gonna go and I pick you up after your work. - Alana said.

I don't want Alana to go. It's my first time with a man alone. I am still scared. I still getting nightmares of Zayn. I don't to be alone.

Um. Can you please stay? - I asked her.

Sorry Anusha, but it's important. - she said.

It's okay. Let her go. Otherwise she will be talking nonsense and not let us work properly. - Ahaan said while laughing.

Hahahaha..nice joke. - Alana said while making annoying face.

Okay. You can go but You have to come pick me up. - I said and she okay and then she left leaving me and ahaan alone.

Okay lets go and start the work. - He said.

Okay - I replied.

First Im gonna show you the place and then tell you what I have in my mind for this place. - He said and I nod.

It was a big empty studio right now. But I already have soo many ideas after looking the place. There was a window instead of one wall in this room. From top to bottom. The view was beautiful from there. The light was coming through it and falling on the wall in front.

So this is the place. I want my photo booth in front of this window and also I want a little cabin for myself where I can edit my photos. And also I want the little design on the wall next to the window. And do whatever else you want to do. - He said.

This place is so good and I already have so many ideas for this place. And also I will take care all the things you want for this place. - I said.

Okay I'm so excited for how this turn out later. Can you share what's in your mind. - He asked.

Ofcourse. Umm..let's start with this wall. On this entire wall we will make all the things related to photography. We can do make paintings there or also we can also put up some posters. And In that corner, we gonna make your little and cabin and on the other side there will be your photo booth. And also we need curtain for this wall. If you don't want lights for your photography you can use curtains. - I gave him whole description of what I'm gonna do.

Amazing. I love the Idea. So when will you start the work? - He asked.

From today. I need pictures of this place and the whole map. So I can decide what needs to be made in how much space. And then

I can make the 3d description of this place. After that you can start the labour work. - I said.

Okay that's sound good. I'm gonna share all the details to you. - He said.

So that's it. It's a wrap. - I said while smiling.

Okay thanks. Let's go for coffee? - He asked.

Umm..I have to goo...

Ohh come on. Let's go. It will take time to Alana to come. Till then let's have coffee. - He said cutting me in middle of conversation.

Okay let's go. - I said.

I text Alana to come and she said it will take 30 minutes to come. We do downstairs and there's a small cafe near the building. We ordered the coffee and he started the conversation again.

So, where did you study from? - He asked.

Russia. - I replied.

Then why here? - He asked.

My family is here. My brother and my sister-in-law. They wants me to stay with them. So I'm here. And your studio is my first project. - I said.

Okay nice. But It doesn't seem like you are doing it for the first time. You look professional. - He said.

Thank youu. - I replied.

Our conversation go very well and I'm so proud of myself right now that I am finally coming out of my shell and starts making friends. Alana came after 30 minutes. And she text me to come outside.

Ahaan listen. Alana has arrived so I have to go now. - i said. And we both got up and go outside where Alana is standing outside the car. I stand next to her say bye to Ahaan.

I didn't realise where the time flies while talking to you. It's so good to talk to you. Hope we meet soon. - He said while blushing.

Yeah same here. We'll meet soon. - I replied and say bye to him. He winks at me and goes.

Ohh my god. Are you guys flirting? - she said while teasing me.

No. There's nothing like that Alana. - I said while blushing.

Umm hmmm..something something - she teased again.

Noooo. Nothingggggggg. - I said while glaring at her.

We both sat down in the car and talked about all the stuff, work, his studio,my ideas and ofcourse Ahaan.He's cute but I am not ready for man in my life. I still have to get out of my old pain and memories.

We reached home in the evening. I skipped lunch for work and also because of traffic. And I'm so hungry right now so I decided to go to that library cafe near me. I called Alana for asking to go with me and but she already had lunch while she goes for work. So I decided to go alone.

I go there and the place was so crowded as there were lot's of people. I saw a table empty and sit there and ordered pasta and coffee for me. And started reading a book which was already kept open on the table. I started reading the book, It was an autobiography. - A man of honour by Joseph Bonanno.

What the fuck is this book about- I said to myself because I was not understand the book.

It's an autobiography of Mafia written by the biggest mafia itself. A dark and deep voice came from behind. I turned around and saw a Man with devilish look standing. And i started thinking where I have seen him before?

And by the way you are sitting in my table. - He said and his deep voice brought me back to my senses.

Oh I'm really sorry. I thought this is empty. I will leave. - I said while standing up.

No. Sit with me. There is no other table empty here. - he said in his comanding voice and I just sat down. I don't know what happened to me.

After that he sat across me and started reading his book and then waiter came with my order. And I started eating silently and I'm still wondering that where I have seen him before.

I have never seen you here before. Are you new here? - He asked and I choked because I was in my thoughts.

Yeah sorry... Im new here. - I said while coughing.

He passed the glass of water towards me and I drank the water. Now I'm good.

So where did you come from? - He asked again.

Russia. - I replied.

Interesting. Why here? - He asked again.

Family. And by the way you asked a lot of questions.- I replied.

I know. Only then we will able to know each other. - He replied with smrink.

And why do we have to know each other? - I asked.

Now who's asking questions? - he said.

I smiled and he smiled with me. And ohh god his smile...it's so sexy and pretty. He is the most handsome man I ever saw. But still I didn't remember that where I have seen him before, and now I couldn't bear it anymore so I asked him.

Okay One more question. - I said.Why do I feel like I've seen you somewhere before?

I have been to Russia many times , you may have seen me there. - He replied.

Why? Why have you been to russia so many times? - I asked again.

And you told me that I was asking questions. - He said while looking deeply in my eyes.

If you don't want to tell then It's ok. - I replied with hesitation.

Business. - He said.

Ohh.. what business do you do? - I asked again and then he laughed and I made my annoying face.

Umm..import export. - He said.

And when he said import export I immediately remembered who is he. My heart skipped a beat. I was so terrified of what Alana said about him and what my google search said. But still I managed to say.

What do you import or export? Arms? Drugs or Humans? - I said and immediately regretted.

So you finally remembered who am I? - he said while sitting straight on the chair.

Yeah finally. You are.....Farhaad...Mirza. - I said hesitatly.

Chapter 16

Farhaad POV-

Today was a very tiring day. I need to take a rest, and rest does not mean sleeping, I need a good fuck. So I called one of my whore, she's actually a daughter of one of my client and she thought that sleeping with me can make me fall in love with her, but that's not true. She's nothing but a whore to me. Sleeping with man or doing all nasty things can never make anyone fall in love. I called her and asked her to come to my penthouse. And she agreed to come.

I always just used women according to my needs. And I threw them away when I got bored with them until her. My Angel.Ever since I saw her I have been crazy about her. But when Jibraan said that she's Kabir's sister, I tried to forget her. I tried really hard to forget her because how can I fall in love with my enemy's sister.I kept myself busy with work So that I stop thinking about her but nothing like that happened. As much as I want to forget her, I missed her smiling and innocent face so much. I don't know how long I will be able to control myself.

I was thinking all this while driving and suddenly I saw her passing through the side of my car. I immediately stopped my car and saw her through my side view mirror to know that Is she real or I'm so crazy that I can see her?

But it's not my imagination, she's here. Maybe its my Destiny that all the big cities in India and she had to come here, so close to me.

Now I could no longer control myself So I got out of the car and started following her. She's with her friend or something, they got into a library cafe and I saw her through the window, she was talking with her friend. She looks happy, last time when I saw her she was so terrified because of that incident in the club. But now she looks so cute while smiling and talking and playing with her long hairs. I just can't stopped looking at her.

How someone can be so beautiful? - I said to myself.

I literally just kept looking at her for more than 2 hours while standing outside. When she started coming out of the cafe I hid myself so I can follow her without her knowledge.

She was going to the same direction as my penthouse. Maybe she lives near me and I smrinked at that thought. While walking down the streets she pointed towards my building, maybe she wanted to know that whom does this building belongs?

Oh my Angel....When I take you to the same penthouse and Fuck you in my bed, You'll find out who does it belong to and who does you belong to.

- I said this to myself and the only thought of fucking her makes me so hard. What will happen when she is gonna actually lying under me with her legs wrapped around my waist.

But she looks so fragile and innocent. I'll afraid that I might hurt her. I'm Devil..how can I be gentle with her? How will I do? How will I be gentle for her. I have to learn and she's gonna teach me how to be gentle.

After walking for 15 minutes they finally reached there building. She really lives so close to me. This is seriously my fucking destiny that she is this close to me. Now It's easy for me to stalk her to see her and when the time comes I'm gonna talk to her.

After seeing her address I came back to my car and goes to my penthouse. I lived on the 15th floor. I owned this whole building. When I enter the penthouse I immediately goes to my room, I need to release myself.

When I opened the door, I saw a sexy girl lying on my bed in the hot red lingerie . I totally forgot about her that I called her. She stands up and came close to me and started seducing me.

I tried to tell her that Im not in the mood right now. My mood had changed since I saw Anusha. Now I don't want to fuck any whore. But she still go down on me and started unbuckling my belt.

She took out my dick and shoved it in her mouth. Her method of blowing me was amazing. I sat down on bed and she was kneeling in front of me and blowing me. Now I couldn't help it and I grabbed her by her hairs and shoved my cock deep into her mouth. I forced her head up and voluntarily pushed her head as deep as She could possibly go and began to gag. By doing all that she pushed me over the edge and I couldn't hold myself back any further. I squirted cum heavily into her mouth and she swallowed every inch of it.

After that she wants more but I don't want anything else. I told her to leave and she left upset.I seriously can't help myself right now, when I was fucking her face, I was imagining Anusha instead of her. I was imagining how will she look when she has my dick in her mouth. I was imagining fucking. She will be the death for me.

I immediately called Jibraan. I need to see anusha, I want to know where she goes and when. He picked up the call.

I want you to do something for me. - I said.

Anything for you brother. Tell me how many people I have to kill? - He asked in his agressive voice.

I don't want you to kill anyone but you have to save my life. Because I will die without her. - I said.

What?? Who? - He asked in confusion.

Anusha...My Angel. - I replied.

Are you crazy? Do you understand what you have said? If Kabir came to know about all this then civil war will start between us. A lot of people will die. Kabir would never want you to come even close to her sister's shadow. - He said in one breath and I know he is angry with me but I seriously can't live without her.

Fuck Kabir Malik...If he comes between me and my Angel, I will kill him. - I replied angrily.

Ohh nice and then what will happen when Anusha finds out that you have killed her brother? Will she still love you? - He asked.

She will have to love me..either willingly or by force. It will be her wish. But now I want her. We will see it only when Kabir comes to know about it. - I said.

I don't know what's so special about her that makes you so crazy. Tell me what to do? - He asked.

Find her phone number and tap the phone and connect it to my system. I want to hear all her phone calls, messages and everything. - I said.

Give me 2 days. I'll do it. - he said and cut the call.

Next day I go to the same cafe again at the same time in hope of seeing her again. But this time I'll decide to go inside, the place was so crowded there is only table left so I sit there and started reading an autobiography. Suddenly my phone rang, It was Jibraan, he called me to tell some arrangements he did for Russian Arms deal and he needs me there. So I decided to go to my office but when I came back I saw her sitting on my table. This is truley my fucking destiny.

I decided to go there and talk to her. She was so terrified while talking to me. But I think she knows who I am but she couldn't recall. She looks so beautiful and innocent while talking, smiling, eating. She's just perfect.

Suddenly she recalls where she's been seen me.

You aree...Farhaad....Mirza. - She said with hesitation.

Yes I am.. Farhaad Mirza. And why are you scared of me? I'm not gonna do anything to you. - I said.

Ofcourse. Mr. Mafia, Why would you do anything to me...I have not done any harm to you..- she said that in hindi and she looks so cute while speaking hindi but her accent was different and she gave me a nickname of Mr. Mafia.

Oh..so you know how to speak hindi..Nice. And yes tumme kch nahi bigada so don't be scared Angel.- I said while laughing.

Angel? - she asked with doing her eyebrows up.

If you can call me Mr. Mafia then can't I call you Angel? - I asked.

She hesitates again and want to speak but had no words and then she finally speaks.

I will have to go now. It's late. - She said while standing up.

Okay. See you soon Angel. - I said and then she leaves.

Chapter 17

Anusha POV-

When he calls me Angel, I feel something in my heart. Nobody ever give me any nickname except Zayn, he called me Babydoll which still disgust me.I just stood up and went out from there.

I reached home after 10 minutes of walking, when I got text from shazia that she is coming over for dinner. Shazia had kept a maid for me, Priya. She cooks very delicious food for me.

Shazia came at 8pm and hugs me tightly. We are meeting after so many days. We sat on dining table and start having coversations and food.

So, what's new in your life? - She asked.

Umm..I meet Alana's friend Ahaan today. And I'm all ready to start the work. It's feel so good being independent. - I replied and I didn't tell her about Farhaad, because I thought she will get tensed.

Wow that's good. I'm so proud of you. - She replied with smile.

Umm..how's Kabir bhaiya? - I asked.

Well he's good and busy at his office and surprisingly he asked about you. - She said.

I was in totally shocked when she said he asked about me. I'm so emotional and happy right now.

What did he asked? - I asked with excitement.

Nothing much but he asked that how will things with you now and Are you comfortable here or not? - She said.

He even asked this much is enough for me. - I replied with smile.

You know, you should visit home. Have dinner with us. Maybe Kabir started talking to you. Like who knows what happen. - She said.

Yeah I can give it a try. I'll come home after I come when I finish Ahaan's work. - I said.

Ohh so his name is Ahaan. Nice name. - She said.

Oh no..not you please. Alana already bothering me on this topic. I just met him once. - I replied annoyingly.

Okay okay. I won't bother you. But you have to tell me if something happens. Promise? - She said.

Promise. - I replied.

Then we both laughed and eat our dinner. It's already 11pm now and Shazia left because Kabir must have come home. I decided to sit in the balcony after doing my night routine and changing into night clothes. I sat there and started looking at Farhaad's building. I could see that top floor lights were open, maybe he lives there. I forgot to ask him where he lives.

I was lost in my thoughts when my phone suddenly beeps. It was a text from Ahaan.

Awake? - He texted.

Yes. - I replied.

I'm gonna send you photos of studio which you have asked for. Then you can start doing your work. He texted again.

Oh yeah. Sure. - I replied.

He send me all the photos of studio which I want. From tomorrow I can start doing work on his studio. I need 2-3 days for making a map of everything.

How many days it will take? - He asked.

2-3 days. I text you when it's done. - I said.

Okay good. Can I ask you something? - He asked again.

I was curious what's he gonna ask. Maybe he's going to ask me for a date. I texted yes and he replied exactly the same thing which I was thinking.

Can we meet tomorrow for coffee or something?Ofcourse if you are free?

Oh god whyy, why god. You know I'm not ready for this. What can I do now? - I said to myself loudly.

I immediately texted Alana for help. Because seriously I don't know what to do. One side of me saying me to say yes to him and come out of bubble and the other side is scaring me for what happened to me before.

Listen Alana. I need help. - I texted.

Yes. What happened??? - she replied immediately.

Ahaan asked me for coffee or something. What should I say to him? - I said.

Say yes girllll.. he's the best. - Alana replied.

But I think I'm not ready for this. What should I do? - I asked her again.

Okay girl. If you are not ready just say no but if you trust me then you should say yes.- she replied.

I said okay. Maybe I should give it a try. How long will I remain in this bubble? I should free myself from all my fears. I have to be strong.

I texted Ahaan.

Okay. We can go tomorrow. - I said yes to him with all my courage.

Perfect. I'll pick you up tomorrow at 5pm. - He replied.

Done. - I said.

Farhaad POV-

Jibraan texted me that he found anusha's number and he also hacked her phone. So now I can see all her conversations and hear all her calls. I know it's creepy but I am also a pshyco for her. I know he said 2 days but I literally forced Jibraan to do that as fast as he can.

I opened that system in my phone through some app. On that app I can see and hear all her conversations.

Suddenly a message appeared on my that app,someone texted Anusha. My blood boiled when that motherfucker asked her for a date. She was in confusion so she asked her friend and she approved.

He's not gonna able to go on date with my Angel. I will kill him before that. - I said to myself.

I extracted all the information of that Ahaan. He's opening his photography studio and anusha is working on his studio as an interior designer. He going to coming tomorrow to pick her up but he won't be able to do that. I have a plan.

Chapter 18

Farhaad POV

I was so fucking angry and jealous because of that fucker asking my angel for date. And she also said yes. I need to destroy him. And I have a plan.

At same night I goes to his building in which his studio is. I already hacked all the cameras here so, no one would know what happened. I wore black tracksuit with gloves and helmet so no one would recognise me.

I sneak inside the building, the guards were sleeping. I would never hire such guards, who sleeps on duty. I went on his floor and opened the door of his studio with a bang. I came here with a container of kerosene oil in my hand. I'm gonna burn his studio and he is very lucky that he is not here right now. Or I would have burnt him alive with this studio.

I poured kerosene on all four walls of his studio. And standing on the door of his studio. I threw the lighter towards his studio. The place caught fire immediately. A lot of construction stuff was also kept there. I burnt that too.

I saw the whole studio burning in front of my eyes. And that gives me a lot of peace. I took out my phone from my pocket and texted Ahaan with my private number.

If you are seen anywhere near her again, Next time I will burn youu instead of your studio..SHE IS MINE.MY ANGEL.

I get out of the building and stand across of the building. Fire fighters and ambulances started coming. There are chaos all around the street. Everbody was evacuating the building. There was people running around.

Look Angel what I had to do because of you. My love.I said this to myself.

Anusha POV-

Today I'm going on a date with Ahan. I'm so nervous right now. I don't know what to wear, how to act. And also I have to start the work on Ahaan's studio also. There are so much chaos in my mind right now.

Suddenly my door bell rang again and again. I immediately go and open the door. There was Alana standing and panicking alot.

What...what happened Alana? Are you alright? - I asked her.

Anusha...just...turn on the news on T.V. - She said.

I also panicked and immediately opened the news channel and jaw dropped in horror. The news was on every channel that the building is burned down by someone. It was the same building in which Ahaan studio was. I also started panicking and pick up my phone and started calling Ahaan.

After 3-4 rings, he picks up.

Hey Ahaan..are you alright? I just saw the news. What happened? - I asked in panic.

Everything is over Anusha. And please don't call me again. I never wanted to talk to you or meet you. Never contact me again. Or he will also burnt me alive like he did to my studio- He said and before I could speak he cuts the call.

What happened? What did he say? - Alana asked.

I don't know what happened. He said that don't call or meet again. And before I could speak he cuts the call. - I replied in confusion.

I didn't tell Alana the whole thing, because I myself could not understand what he said. Who's going to burn him? What was he talking about. This is so much confusing.

Maybe he's in worried right now. We should give him some time. - She said.

Yeah. You are right. - I replied.

We calmed down ourselves and I gave water to Alana and after that she leaves from my house. I was so heartbroken right now because of what happened to Ahaan and his studio. I know he was so excited for his studio and also that now I'm unemployed again and also my date is cancelled. And also who was he? I called Ahaan again and again for asking him about him. Who was he talking about? But he didn't pick up my call.

Suddenly my phone beeps. I saw in hope that it was Ahaan but it was shazia. She texted me to say All the best for my date and my work.

I told her everything that happened and she is also worried now.

I'm sorry Anusha for what happened. Are you fine. - Shazia texted.

Yes I'm all right but little worried for Ahaan. - I texted back.

You know what..Just come home for tonight. Here you feel relaxed with me. And also your mind will get diverted by coming here. - She texted.

But? - I replied.

Kabir is also not in the country. Please Anusha come na.- she replied.

Okay. I'm coming. - I replied.

Okay I'll send the car in one hour. Get ready. - She replied.

I reached to shazia's place in the evening. We sat in the garden with tea in our hands. And started talking. I told her everything what happened in detail but I didn't tell her about that confusing incident. I let go that thing go from my mind and changed the subject of talking.

So How's Kabir Bhaijaan? And where is he? - I asked.

Umm..Anusha I'm so sorry but I lied to you. He's in the office and he will there with us at dinner. - she said.

Why? Why did you lie to me? - I asked.

Because if I had not lied, you would not have come. - she said.

But if Kabir sees me here, he will get angry again.Maybe I should go back. - I said in annoying voice.

No. You are not going back. You are staying here for tonight. - she said.

Even If I tried to force her to let me go, she wouldn't agree so I said yes. And deep down I'm praying that Kabir should not get angry after seeing me there.

At night when Kabir gets home, I was sitting on the kitchen counter while shazia was cooking food and we were talking. We didn't saw Kabir watching us.Suddenly my eyes fell on him and I stopped talking. Shazia also turned around to see Kabir, he was standing there with so much anger in his eyes. God knows what happened next.

(What will happen when Anusha get to know about who burned the building? Did Anusha and Ahan ever gonna meet again? What will Kabir do now after seeing Anusha in his house again?)

Stay tuned to know more.Vote, share, comment.Please please comment and tell me how's the story. Thankyou.Love yaa...❌

Chapter 19

K abir POV-

I was tired of work today. After the deal with the russians canceled, I focused all my attention on Germany deal. This Germany deal is of Farhaad but If he can steal my clients from me then so can I.

And also I still can't believe that Mr. Zayn died by an accident, something definitely happened that was not revealed. This thing doesn't let me sleep at night. So I contacted the Russian police again. I asked them to investigate again. And they are ready to do. Hopefully this time something will definitely come out. I know Anusha has done something which she is hiding. I also asked them to investigate Anusha's nanny again. She definitely know something about that night.

I came out of my thoughts when my phone rings. It was Imraan, I picked up the call and he asked me something about deal and when I am leaving the office? I looked at my watch and tell him that I was just leaving. He said okay and cuts the call.

I took the elevator to the parking lot and started walking towards my car. I was all alone.

Suddenly a man came out of nowhere. I can't see his face it was covered with mask. I tried to make conversation with him.

Who do you want? Who sent you?- I asked.

Your death sent me to kill you. - He replied.

I wish killing me was this easy. - I replied with small laugh and folding up my sleeves.

I looked at him with fierce eyes and he also clenched his fists and glared me. The fight erupted suddenly, He threw a powerful punch at me but I ducked and threw a quick jab in his ribs. He grunted, his face contorted in pain, but he quickly recovered. He swinged again with another punch but I dodged it again and and thew a sharp kick to his stomach.

If someone had to kill me, then atleast send a good fighter. - I said to him with smrink while he was laying on ground breathing hardly.

He stood up after hearing me and I was also ready to fight him. But suddenly He pulled out a gun from his pocket and aimed at me.

I used to play with these toys in my childhood. - I said.

He shot at me but I ducked and jumped towards my car and hide behind it. I know he was coming towards me from the right side. And that's all what I want. When he comes to the right side I stood up and held his hand and twisted it. He screamed in pain and the gun fell down. I turned towards him and gave him a smack. He fell on the ground, I picked up his gun and pointed towards him.

Tell me. Who the fuck sent you or I will kill you.- I roared in anger.

Even If I told you, you will still kill me. - He said.

And if you don't tell me, First I will torture you and then killed you. It would be better to tell and die an easy death. - I said to him.

Farhaad Malik. - He said.

My blood boiled in anger after listening his name. But it's not his style to sent a killer to kill me. I know this much about him that if he wants to kill me, then he will kill me with his own hands.

Lie - I said and shot him in his head. He died instantly. But what if he was saying truth. What if really Farhaad sent him?

I immediately called Imraan and asked him to come to parking lot. He came after 15 minutes and he stunned after he saw dead body in front of his eyes.

Who was he? - he asked.

Someone sent him to kill me. Maybe Farhaad. - I said.

If he can do this, then we should also attack him. - he said in anger.

No. Not now. First I have to confirm whether this is correct or not. Because I know this is not his style. - I said.

But? What if this is true? - He asked.

Then he will have to pay the price. - I said and tell him to get rid of the body. And I left for home. I know Shazia was waiting for me. I won't tell her anything about this.

I reached home, and go inside and saw Anusha sitting on the kitchen counter talking to shazia. I was already in so much anger and there she is pouring kerosene in my anger.

What the hell she is doing here? - I asked shazia.

She's here for the dinner. She will go back tomorrow. - She said and I ignored her and goes to my room.

I got freshen up and go downstairs, Shazia and Anusha already sitting in their chairs and was waiting for me. I sat down and started eating, Shazia made wonderful Biryani tonight. She cooks amazing. Then suddenly I saw Anusha, she was eating Biryani with her hands like Dad used to eat. My heart aches looking at her.

Suddenly she feels my eyes on her, I immediately look away. She's just like Dad.

After eating I went to the garden for little walk. And also I need to talk to Farhaad about that incident. I decided to call him.

What happened Kabir? You have started missing me alot these days? - He said with laugh.

I was attacked by someone in my office parking lot. And when I asked him that Who sent you. He told me your name. I swear Farhaad if it's you then remember I'm gonna kill with my own bare hands. - I said in anger.

Wait..waittt..why would I sent someone to kill you? I will do this auspicious work with my own hands. - He said while teasing me.

Why would he lie even while dying? - I asked.

Ask his soul... And one more thing, I'm not coward that I will send someone else to kill you. - He said and I know he's saying truth because sending someone to kill me is not his style. Someone definitely want war between us.

Fine. - I replied and cuts the call.

After little walk and talking to Farhaad I went inside the house to my study room. When I entered I saw Anusha standing in front of large portrait of my parents. I felt that she was crying after looking at Dad's photo. I faked coughed and she turned around. I don't know what the fuck happened to me after seeing her crying. Same thing happened last time too.

Can you tell me anything about Dad? - she said and starting walking towards me.

What do you want to know? - I asked her and immediately realised what the fuck I just said.

Anything. Just tell me. - She said.

He was kind, caring, hardworking. He was ready to help anyone who needs any help in whatever way he could. - I said these lines and stopped talking when I realised that I also forgot lots of things about him.

Anusha also started crying. I got little emotional too. And suddenly she said something which I felt from day one.

But all three of us have same nose. - she said smiling at me.

I smiled at her too. What the fuck????

Will you ever gonna treat me as your sister? If Dad were alive, He would have also wanted us to live together happily - She asked and caught me off guard.

Never. Just tell me what the fuck do you want to leave us alone. - i asked and the old kabir is back.

I already told you hundreds of times that I don't want anything from you. I just want all of us together. I want family. I want you Bhaijaan. I never had a family. I never had loved by someone.- she said in anger.

What about Zayn? He was your family. - I said.

He was not my family. He was a fucking mons....She stopped speaking in middle of sentence and ran away while crying.I didn't understand what was she saying. Suddenly my phone beeps and I received the text message from the russian police.

You were right. We found something. - Officer texted.

Chapter 20

Anusha POV-

I was already so much distressed about what happened to Ahaan and then my job. And on top of that Kabir was scolded me. I told him hundreds of times that I don't want anything from him but he won't listen to me.

I started crying and ran away from there. I ran away from his house. I was just kept walking away, After a while when I regained control on myself. Then I saw that I reached the beach, I realised that I had been walking for more than 15 minutes. I decided to sit on the beach for a while. It was almost midnight and there was no one on the beach.

I was watching the waves of water coming towards me. The moonlight was falling on the waves of water.There was lot of peace there and I felt very relaxed.

But suddenly, I heard some mens talking and coming towards me. I got scared a lot. I stood up and started walking away from there. But those four people immediately stood in a circle around me.

What do you want? - I asked them.

You. - one of them replied.

I knew I was in big trouble, the smell of alcohol was coming from these people and they also had bottles in their hands. I got scared but still I gathered all mu courage and pushed one of them and started running to save my life. They were also running behind me. I didn't even know where I was running.

Suddenly two hard hands pulled me into an small alley. I thought one of them found me and I was about to scream when he put his hand on my mouth.

Sshhhhh...It's me Angel - He whispered in my ear and I literally rolls my eyes back at the sensation of his breath against my neck.

I've got you my Angel - He said again.

At first I didn't understand, but when he called me Angel, I understood who he was.

If I remove my hand, Are you going to scream? - He asked me and his breath on my neck giving me different type of feelings.

I nodded my head in No. and he slowly removes his hand and turned me around. I was in total shock right now. How did he know where I was? There was so many questions in my mind.

You stay here and I will come in just 5 minutes - He said again.

When he started leaving I caught hold of his collar and stopped him.

Please...don't.... leave me...alone...I don't know what they will do to me... - I said while sobbing hardly.

Just trust me..No one can touch My Angel as long as I am alive. - He said in threatening voice.

But I still holding his collar and wasn't ready to leave him. So he hugged me. He hugged me like his life was depended on me. He buried his face in my neck, his one hand was caressing my hair and other hand was on my waist holding me tight.

When he hugged me I felt like heaven. Someone hugged me so lovingly for the first time. I hugged him back, I hugged him so tight and started crying. Because of so much crying and tiredness I started loosing my consciousness. Suddenly he said something and I felt safe in his arms.

You have me..All of me..Till the day I die.. I AM THE DEVIL...I will protect you My Angel...- He said and I lost my consciousness in his arms.

Farhaad POV-

After burning his studio and threatening him, I thought that Anusha will come to cafe today. So I decided to go there but suddenly my phone beeps, it was Anusha's phone message.

Kabir's wife invited Anusha to her house. She was going there. I have to live another day without seeing her. After that small talk in cafe, It was so hard for me to controll myself. I want to see her again, talk to her again. But it's okay I'll wait until she's all mine.

At night suddenly my phone rings, It was Kabir. He told me about the attack on him and also said that I send someone to kill him. That's not my fucking style, I'm not coward. But it was a trick played by someone so that he can lit the fire between us. I need to find out who's ruining my name. I have to meet Kabir.

I was missing my Angel so much, suddenly I saw movement in Anusha's location. She was running somewhere at late night. I quickly sat inside my car and started moving towards her location. I knew something was wrong.

I parked my car in an small alley and started walking towards her. When I reached near her location I saw her running and four people were running behind her. I quickly pulled her in alley and started calm her down. But she was so terrified.

My blood was boiling in anger so much right now that I will burn them alive. They put their hand on what is mine. When I was going to kill them, Anusha grabbed my collar. Till now no one has had the courage to touch me like that, but this girl...She's death to me.She was terrified that I couldn't get away from her. I hugged her.She was melting in my arms like a candle. I buried my face in her neck. Her fragrance was like the fragrance of heaven. I forget the whole fucking world in her arms. She was crying so hard and I was starting to calm her down. But she get unconscious.

I picked her up in my arms and put her in my car. She looked so pale because of fear but what the hell she was doing here at this late?

I reached home and picked her up again and took her to my penthouse. I didn't care if Kabir was searching for her. Tonight she will only be with me. Whatever happens we will see tomorrow morning.

I laid her down on the bed. The moonlight was falling from window on her face. She was looking so beautiful. I couldn't look away. No matter how many times I looked at her but I was not satisfied.

I called my maid and told her to change the clothes of Anusha. I gave her my oversized hoodie and walked out of the room.The maid came out and said that she changed her clothes. I go back inside and saw her laying on my bed. My maid opened her long mermaid hairs which was scattered on my bed. My hoodie was coming up to her thighs in which her legs were visible. She's truly an angel. Angel who is in the grip of the Devil.

Suddenly I saw something unusual, I came close to her legs and saw fainted scars on her legs. Like someone scratched her. I was in so much confusion right now. What happened to her? How did these scars come? Did someone hurt her?

Well whatever I asked her in the morning. I lay next to her and cagged her in my arms. I started moving my fingers on her face and remove her hair from her face which was troubling her.

Soon Angel..You will be laying naked on my bed and I will be inside you. - I whispered this in her ears and sleep while hugging her.

Chapter 21

Anusha POV-

No...please..leave mee...please...stay away from me...please...stayy..awayyy...

I woke up with screaming. I was panting heavily. Suddenly I realised it was just a nightmare. This nightmare of Zayn came after very long time. Maybe because of what happened last night.

Waitt...What the hell happened last night??Then slowly I started remembering everything from last night.I looked around me and found myself in unfamiliar place. Suddenly I realised that someone is watching me. I looked at him and remembered everything that how he helped me last night.

Where am I? - I asked him.

In my bed..In my home. - He replied.

His dark black eyes were looking at deep in my eyes. He was looking so handsome while sitting on the sofa.

You fainted last night so I bought you home. - He said again.

Where's my phone? My sister-in-law must be worried about me. - I asked him while searching my phone.

Don't worry. I already told her that you are at home. You explain her futher by yourself. - He replied.

What? But how did you unlock my phone? - I asked in confusion.

I am a hacker too. - He replied with wink.

I need to go back. - I said while standing up from the bed and realised that I was not wearing my clothes.

What the fuck...who changed my clothes? - I asked angrily.

Me. - he replied and I can see the lust in his eyes.

I went near him angrily. He was sitting on the sofa and I stood in front of him.

Why? How dare you to touch me? - I yelled at him.

Suddenly he pulled my hands and made me sit in his lap. My legs were on either side of his waist. Suddenly I realised that I'm not wearing any bra. Oh god? What else could he have done?

Don't..you..daree..to yell..at..me..UNDERSTAND? Or I will punish you and you will beg me to stop. - He said in threatening voice near my lips.

Leave me. - I tried standing up from his lap but he cagged me in his arms. He was so strong and I am unable to free myself from his cage. I took a deep breath and gave up trying to free myself. I started looking down on his lap. He held my chin and turned my face up.

Tell me, Angel.- He said slowly in my ears.What? - I asked.

Tell me everything that happened to you. - He said and I know what he was talking about. I'm sure He saw me screaming while I was having that nightmare.

Why there are scars on all over you body? What happened to you? What was that nightmare? Who hurt my Angel?- He asked lot of questions.

You asked so many questions. - I replied slowly.

He gave a small smile and asked again.

Nothing happened. It was just a nightmare. Now please leave me. I have to go. - I replied but he won't ready to leave me instead of leaving me he hold me more tightly.

Tell me Why I can't stop thinking about you? Hmm? What the fuck did you do to me? - He said and pulled me close.

I had very strange feelings while he was holding me. I never wanted to go away from his arms. I felt very safe in arms but also so scared. He is The Devil.What if he also turned out to be like Zayn?

I don't know what are you talking about. Just leave me please. - I said.

You know what I'm talking about. Look into my eyes and tell me what you see? - He said in his commanding voice and I looked into his deep black devilish eyes with fear.

I'm scared..please leave me. - I said with small tears running on my face from my eyes.

Ohh Angel..you don't have to be scared of me. - He said while wiping my tears.

Look, I'm not a nice man. I'm not a fucking hero. And I won't pretend. But What I am is someone who will slaughter your demons one by one untill you are finally free of them. I LOVE YOU ANGEL. You are the fire to my icey heart. And I won't stop untill you are fully.throughly.and undeniably MINE. - he said and I literally had a panic attack and more tears started running out of my eyes.

I...wanna...go..home. - I said while sobbing so hard.

He stood up while holding me same position. My legs were wrapped around his waist and my hands were wrapped around his neck. And when he stood up I buried my face in his neck and started sobbing so hard.

He opened the washroom door and he made me sit on the slape near the sink. I let go of him after sitting on the slape. He put my hairs behind my ear and wiped my tears.

Show me your scars - He said.

But Why? - I asked.

I want to see how many times you needed me and I wasn't there for you. - He whispered.

He puts his hand on my thigh and then he grabbed the bottom part of my hoodie. And then he took off my hoodie. I was just in my underwear in front of him. He was touching my entire body with his eyes, but this time it was not lust. It was love and an ache in his heart.

I still have some fainted scars on my collar bones, on my shoulders, breasts and on my stomach. He started moving his index fingers on my shoulder and collar bone scars. I can feel his fingers shivering on my skin and I can clearly saw the pain and anger in his eyes.

Then he turned around and picked towel from wardrobe and wrapped it around me. I was still crying and again he came closed near me.

WHO.DID.THIS.TO.YOU? I'll bury him alive in the ground.- He asked in anger.

I looked up at him and said.

You won't have to do this. I already did.- I said proudly with smile.

What do you mean? - He asked me in confusion.

Nothing.- I replied.

He gave me his devilish smile.

So you're not as innocent as I thought. - he said.

And then he leans in, so carefully. Heart beating between us and he's so close, he's so close that I can't feel my legs anymore. I can't feel my fingers or the cold or anything of this room because all I feel is him, everywhere , filling everything and then he whispers near my lips.

Please Angel.

I closed my eyes and then he kisses me.

His lips are softer than anything I've ever known, soft like snowfall, like biting into cotton candy. It's sweet, it's so effortlessly sweet.

And then it changes.

He bit my lower lip and I moaned in his mouth while kissing him. Aahhhh...slowly please.

He broke the kiss and looked deep into my eyes. I started biting my lower lip and then he kisses me again.This time stronger, desperate like he has to have me, like he's dying to memorize the feel of my lips against his own. The taste of him is making me crazy.

But suddenly I came back into my senses. I realised that he is underworld mafia. He is the devil. How can I love him? What if Kabir and shazia gets to know about this? Kabir's gonna be so furious and what if he sends me back to Russia?

I broke my kiss and pushed him away. He was breathing like he's lost his mind.He again came close to me and want to kiss me but I stopped him.

Don't - I said and his jaw locked and then he stared at me with his empty eyes.

Don't what? - He asked flatly.What's wrong Angel? - He again asked.

I don't - I started talking and took a deep breath before saying - I don't want to fall in love with you.It wasn't a statement as much as it was a plea.

You don't seem to have much choice. - He answered.

I get up from the slape and I saw my clothes kept on a wardrobe. I changed in my clothes immediately. He saw me changing my clothes but didn't said anything.

I want to go home. - I said.

When will you come to meet me again? I want to know who did this to you.- He said.

Never, I'm not gonna meet you again and I already told you. You won't have to do anything. Please just drop me home. - I said while pleading him.

You won't be able to get rid of me easily. I'm The Devil and you my angel, you are my personal hell and God help me, I don't want to fucking leave.He said and I know I fucked up.

Chapter 22

Farhaad POV-

I lied to her that I changed her clothes. I was joking but I didn't know that she would be so serious about that. When I saw scars on her naked body, my blood boiled in anger. I know something very bad had happened with my Angel. Someone did this to her. But she didn't tell me. My hearts aches when I saw her crying. I just wanted to take away all her sorrows.

When I pulled her in my lap and take her to washroom and saw her scars, I was angry with myself that I didn't there for her when she needed me the most.

And when I kissed her it feels like I'm diving into an ocean of emotion and I'm too swept up in the current to realize I'm drowning and nothing even matters anymore. Not my worries about who or what I am and what I might become. This is the only thing that matters.This.This lips.This moment.

I told her my feelings but she was not ready for this. But it's okay I'm ready to wait. I'll wait for her till eternity. But I need to find what happened to her? I need to talk to her. But she was not telling me the truth. She just wanted to go home. So I dropped her home.

When we got down from the car in front of her building, I tried to talk to her.

Anusha please..give me a chance to show you how much I love you and how much I care about you. - I said in pleading voice.

But she did not listen to me and went to her home without giving me answer. Now I have decided that first I have to win her trust.

It's been weeks since I saw Anusha, she is not even talking to Shazia or Kabir or any of her friends. I checked her messages and calls but she isn't answering any of them.Anusha never talked to kabir on phone or text. I found this very strange that Kabir never texted her to ask her where she is? How is she? I mean he's her brother. But still it's strange.

Suddenly I saw some moments in her location. After weeks she came out of her house today. I need to talk to her. I wanted to see her so badly. So I started following her.

Anusha POV-

When he dropped me home, I was very fed up with all that shit happened to me in just one day. First I had fight with Kabir, then those mens chasing me and then Farhaad. He confessed his feelings to me. He saw my scars, he saw my pain and little bit I think he knows what happened to me. God?? Why, Why my life is so fucked up?

I called Shazia and told her about that fight between me and kabir and thats why I came back to my house. I lied to her. I lied to the one who trusted me the most.All this because of Farhaad, actually not Farhaad it's all because of me. Now I know why Kabir hates me so much. Because I really do spoil everything around me. I told shazia that I need space, because I really am not well. I kept everyone away from me for two weeks.

After two weeks I decided to go out. I searched mall near me. It's 30 minutes away from my house. So I borrowed Alana's car. I was driving after so long but it feels so good. I put on my favourite songs and started enjoying my drive. I reached after 30-35 minutes to the mall, I parked the car in parking and go upstairs.

I decided to shop first. I need new clothes. I go into the Zara store and started wandering around. After 10 minutes of wandering I picked up two dresses, one is white and other is lavender colour. I was so confused in these two dresses, I was looking in the mirror with both dresses on myself. Suddenly my phone beeps and I saw at the screen and my jaw dropped. It was a text message.

Lavender looks perfect on my Angel. - He texted.

I started looking around me with so much curiosity and fear on my face. How's he know where am I? Is he stalking me? Where is he?

I don't care if he's stalking me or not. He thinks that whatever he wants will happen but no. I choosed white dress insted of lavender one. Although I liked lavender but still, I picked white one and goes to changing room.

I entered one of the room and closed the door. And suddenly those two familiar hands grabbed me, he was hiding behind the door. He put one of his hand on my mouth and other on my waist. I tried to push him away but again he was so strong.

When you know you can't escape me so why do you tried? - He whispered against my ears and same sensations runned on my skin.

Now, are you going to scream if I move my hand? - He asked and I nodded in No.

Good girl. - He whispered again and moved his hands from my mouth.

What the fuck are you doing here? How did you know I am here? And why are you always puts your hand on my mouth? - I yelled at him with slow voice.

And someone said that I asked lots of questions. - he said with smrink.

What do you want? - I asked annoyingly.

You. My Angel. - he whispers near my lips.

I already told you that I don't want all this. Please let me go. - I said.

Okay fine. You don't want all this then okay but you have to give me one chance or else I'm gonna stalk you everywhere. Everywhere means Everywhere..Even in your brother's house. - He said slowly coming close to me.

I'm not a girl you can love, and not just you..not one can love me. I ruin everything around me. - I said and tears started forming up in my eyes.

He took a deep breath and said.

I'm already ruined. But if you also leaves me then I will become even more.. - He said in his deep husky voice.

Just leave me please. I'm begging you. Leave me alone. Whatever happened between us in your house, it was a mistake. - I said with tear flowing from my eyes.

Never. I can't...I can't leave you..My Angel.. please try to understand I LOVE YOU.. I'm fucking crazy about you...I Love you Anusha. - he said madly.

Will you still love me if I told you that...I..WAS..RAPED ?? Huhh?? Are you still gonna love me the same? Tell me..give me.. - I was yelling at him and asking him like some mad women.

Suddenly his lips meets mine..he kissed me slowly yet deeply. .and then I pushed him away. He takes few steps back and said-

When you make someone falling in love with the darkest part of you, there is nothing you can do that will scare them away. They will be yours forever because they already love all the fucked up bits and pieces of you. -He said and I can't help myself, I hugged him. I hugged him so tight like my life depends on him. And again he said while hugging me back-

And yes I still love you the same with all my heart.

We hugged even more tighter.

Chapter 23

K abir POV-

When the officer texted me that he found something in the case of Mr. Zayn death, I decided to go to Russia. I told Shazia that a urgent meeting came up. I texted officer Richard Archer and casey Bree who was investigating this cass earlier that I am coming to Russia.

I took flight next day and reached russia at night, I decided to stay at hotel. Next day I go to police station to meet Richard and Casey.

Hello Sir. How are you? How's the flight? - Richard asked.

I'm good and flight was also good. Now please can we get to the point. - I answered him in little annoyance.

Fine...As we told you earlier, In post-mortem reports, we found injuries at two places in his head. One at upper head and other at his lower head. Upper head injury was because of he falls from the stairs but that lower head injury, it was not from falling. - He said and took a little breath and I looked at him with curiosity and gestured him to speak further.

Umm..After your sister left the country and with your permission we scan the whole house. We found some blood stains on the front wall of your sister's bedroom. - He added and took a deep breath to for speak.

Maybe first Anusha pushed him to that wall and after zayn started loosing his consciousness, she pushed him down the stairs and thats why he dies.He said and started looking at me for answer.

Are you sure that this is what happened? - I asked.

Yes sir, after scanning the house and those blood stains, all this points towards murder. And only your sister was there at that time...and ummm..her nanny was there too. - he said.

What about that nanny? Did you investigate her? - I asked again.

No. After your sister left from this country. Her nanny also disappeared. Maybe it was there plan to escape. We are trying to find her but we don't know anything about her yet. - Officer casey added.

I hit the table really hard with my hand and stood up. They also stood up with me and I yelled at them.

God damitt...Find that bitch..I always knew something was wrong. That bitch...she was making us look like a fool by showing her innocent face and her fake tears.

I'm gonna kill that BITCH...Now I'm really gonna kill her.- I yelled at top of my lungs.

They calmed me down. I sat back on chair and take long deep breaths. I can't believe that she did this. And I was most angry with shazia, I always told her that she is not good but I don't know what magic she did on shazia that she never believed me.

Sir...we will find that nanny but...but what about your sister? - Richard asked.

Don't worry about her. I will kill her by myself.- I angrily said that and stood up.

Find that nanny and get the truth out of her that bitch. And I'm going back to India, I have to take care of her. - I told them and got out of station and reached the airport immediately.

I reached India next morning. I decided to go straight to her apartment. I need answers, why did she do that? For money or for me. Maybe she wants to destroy me.

It was 8am maybe and I ranged her door bell. I kept ringing the bell until she opened the door. She was in her nights clothes when I saw her, she was half asleep. She was shocked when she saw me in anger.

Anusha POV-

I was asleep when I heard doorbell. Someone was kept ranging it. I got up from bed and opened the door while I was half asleep. My eyes went open in shock when I saw him in front of me. He was looking so angry. Maybe he find out about Farhaad and me.

Bhaijaan..what happened? Everything's fine? - I asked with all my courage.

You BITCH, what made you think that I wouldn't get to know? - He asked angrily and started coming towards me. He closed the door behind him and I was moving backwards.

What?? Whatt..are youu..talking..about?? I didn't do anything.- I asked again and suddenly I realised that I there is no space behind me and I hit the wall.

Oh..so you didn't do anything? - He started laughing and clapped his hands.

And then he held me by my hairs and looked me with anger and said-

I just came back from Russia. Police said that it was murder. You murdered him. YOU KLLLED HIM..now tell me why? Why the fuck did you do that? You want his money...right?? His money was not enough for you that's why you came here. Right???

Youu..are hurt..ingg me..please I didn't do..anything. - I said while crying. I thought that case was closed but I didn't know that Kabir was still looking into it.He caught me off guard now I don't know what to tell him.

LIE..you are lying again. Answer me youu fucking bitch..why you killed him or else your nanny will going to answer me and I swear to God..I will torture her. - He said and I started crying so heavily. Even I told her to leave the country but what if Kabir finds her.

I'm not lying. Please..leave me..it's hurting. - I said in pleading manner.

So, You won't tell me easily. - He said and before I could think anything he slapped me.He slapped me so hard that I fell on the floor. Blood came out of my lips. And I was again having flashbacks of what zayn did.

He again held me by my hairs and stood me up and again asked me.

Bastard - He yelled at my face and again said - How could you be my sister? Huh..You are just like your mother, your mother tricked my father and ruined our lives. And now you are doing the same. Like mother like daughter... WHORE.

He said and I can't listen this shit about my mother. I know my father loved her. She loved him back. They married with each other. She was not whore.

She was not whore. - I yelled back.

Before he could said anything, his phone rings. He put out his phone and smiled looking at his phone.He picked the call and put in on speaker.

Officer Richard speaking. We found her nanny. - he said on call and my jaw dropped in fear. How could he found her? What will they do to her?

My little sister..is not telling me anything. So please officer..Get the truth out of her nanny. - He said while smiling at me and I started shivering in fear.

And one more thing Officer.. I want her screams to be heard all the way to India. - he said and I started pleading him.

No..noo noo please don't hurt her. She didn't know anything. Please..let her go. - I was pleading in front of Kabir and suddenly I heard her screams. They were beating her brutally.

Okay fine. I'll tell you the truth. But please let her go. - I said again and Kabir tells them to stop and then he cuts the call.

Come on..tell me.. FAST...- He yelled and I started speaking.

I know you're not gonna believe what I'm going to tell you..but it's true. - I said and took a deep breath.

He...he rapped me everyday since I turned 15. It's wasn't always like this. At first he takes care of me like a father, when I grew up his intentions became bad towards me. First he was just harassed me but after sometime he started raping me. And that day also he was doing the same thing.I threatened him that I will tell my brother everything, but he said that he won't be able to do anything. I was trying to find your number to call you. But he caught me...he tried to kill me. I pushed him. I pushed him so hard that his head hit the wall. I didn't want to kill him. I wanted to escape him but he again caught me on stairs. And it was an accident that when I pushed him for saving myself. He slipped from the stairs. I really tried to save him but he was dead. And then I called my nanny. And it was her idea to make it like an accident.

I told him everything in just one breath. I was crying so heavily that I sat down where I was standing. I put myself into ball and crying so badly.

You.. are lying again.. - He said but this time it was not anger, it was sorrow and regret. I looked up deep into eyes and stood up and stopped crying.

I pulled my shirt down from the shoulder and showed him my fainted scars on neck shoulder.

There are many more on my body. Should I show you? - I asked him.

He was so shocked and came close to me, At first I thought he was going to hit me again but he did something which I didn't expect from him. He hugged me.

He hugged me and started crying. Kabir Malik was crying.

I'm so sorry...it was all my fault.. I became blind because of hate..I never think about you..I never asked about youu...It was all my fault. What answer will I give to Dad now? I'm so sorry...sorry..so sorry.

He broked down in my arms and saying sorry. I hugged him back and started crying. Finally he believed me. Although it was not his fault. If I was in his place..I'll do the same.

It was not you fault, bhaijaan. I was the one who delayed in showing courage. I should have killed him long ago. It was not your fault. - I said to him.

And we both hugged and cried for so long.

Now, I will protect you. I'm gonna love you. I will protect my baby sister from everything. Every bad things, I will protect you from every Devil.

He said while hugging me. But when he said the word Devil, I remembered about Farhaad. I'm remembered what happened last night between us. What if Kabir gets to know about that? What if he became the same again.But at this point, I decided to enjoy this moment. I was so happy right now. My brother started loving me. That's all what I want. That's all what I fucking wanted.

I hugged him so hard and we cried.

Chapter 24

arhaad POV-

I already knew when she told me that she was raped, I understood just by looking at those scars. My blood was boiling in anger and I want to torture that bastard who did this to my Angel.

We got out of the mall and goes to parking lot and sat in her car. And I asked her to told me everything.I was so much angry with myself, if I found her earlier maybe I could save her.

She started telling me how her Guardian first molested her and then started raping her daily, how her brother didn't care about her because she's his step sister. How Kabir never paid attention to Anusha.

Now I'm more angry with Kabir. That fucking bastard thought that it was her fault that his dad died. She was not even born at that time. She also lost her parents. What is her fault in this?

But my anger calmed when my Angel told me how she killed that motherfucker. My angel was not as innocent as I thought she was.

I'm gonna Kill your fucking brother. How could he do that? - I said angrily.

No..Noo..Even if he doesn't love or care about me but I do..I do love him and care about him. And because of his wife, I'm here. - she said and calmed me down.

Why don't you tell him all this? He should also realise his mistake. - I said to her.

Of course I want to tell him all this but he doesn't want to talk to me. How can I tell him all this? - She replied.

Unbelievable. How can someone be like this? - I slammed my hand on the steering wheel.

Although I didn't tell anusha that me and her brother are rivals. We fight with each other. Because deep down I know that she loved her brother. And if I told her about our rivalry maybe then she broke off with me because of her brother.

Now It doesn't even matter. I killed him. - she said.

And you did nothing wrong. - I said.

Can you drop me home? - she asked me.

Of course my Angel. - I said and I started the car and drove off from the mall and by the way she picked lavender dress. After reaching her building, I parked the car in parking lot, It was almost night. We both got out of the car.

Would you like to come in for dinner? - She asked and how could I say no.

Ofcourse Angel. - I replied and then we both go upstairs and then she opened the door. I was standing behind her.

When she opened the door. Her maid was there holding glass of water. The glass of water fell from her hand because of fear and then she started shivering while looking at me.

What happened? You are scared as if you have seen a devil? What happened?- Anusha asked her and she looked so cute while speaking hindi in her accent.

Baby, she has seen the devil. That is why she is trembling like this.- I whispered in her ear from behind.

She turned around and gestured me to shut up. And I did what she said. What the hell? This little girl is ruling on me.

Honey, go inside and prepare your dinner.- She goes inside the kitchen while shivering.

Why were you scared her? - She said while folding her hands on her chest.

I did nothing.- I said and hugged her and started kissing her.

After that we had dinner and talked alot about her. We talked about her hobbies, her interests and everything. She was so kind and innocent from her heart. I don't know how I got her. We talked almost for midnight. When I was telling her something, I heard a little snort, she fell asleep on my shoulder while talking to me. I gently caressed her hair and kissed on her forehead. I gently pick her up in bridal style and took her to bedroom and tucked her in bed.When I was leaving her she held my hand in sleep. I sat down on floor on the side of her bed, I kissed on her hand and then put her hands on my eyes and cheeks. I felt so calm and soothing.

I love you my Angel. I'll protect you from everything and every-one. I'll fight the whole world for you. Even If it's your brother. Nobody gonna hurt you. - I whispered to her and left from her house.

Anusha POV-

I woke up with lound bang on door. When I opened the door it was kabir. I told him everything. Now everything is good in my life.

But what about Farhaad? I started to fell in love with him. And now Kabir also behaving good.

He said that he will protect me from every Devil but what about that Devil which I brought home by myself.

We broked our hug and then he wipped my tears and he was constantly saying sorry to me.

Bhaijaan you don't have to say sorry. - I said to him.

It was all my fault that you go through this.- He said.

Let's just forget about that. Let's start fresh. Please.- I said while hugging him again.

You know, just pack your bags. You are coming home with me. - He said and I was on cloud nine but what about farhaad. If I go with him then how I'm gonna meet farhaad.

No. This is my home. I always wanted to be independent. Let me stay here. You can come to meet me whenever you want. - I tried explaining to him and after so much argument he finally understood.

Priya, my maid come to home and she again fell down her stuff on the floor. I asked her again.

what did you see now?- I asked her.

Nothing, madam. I am going inside.- She said and again shivered while going inside.

Kabir left after talking some random stuff with me. And I goes to the kitchen to priya for asking her why she feared with both of them.

Dear. Tell me the truth.. Why were you scared yesterday after seeing Farhad and today after seeing Kabir? - I asked and again she feared.

When you see two devils together, you will definitely get scared..
- She said.

What do you mean, two devils? -I asked her again.

Don't you know? - She said.

Huh?- I asked her.

That the devil whom you brought home yesterday...is Farhad Mirza.. he is a great enemy of your brother...everyone knows this...maybe you don't know it...you have just come, right...I have heard that your father Farhad Mirza's father had a life-threatening situation...since then Farhad is after your brother...to take revenge from him.

Chapter 25

Anusha POV-

I was so much shocked and angry after priya told me about that shit. I'm gonna asked about this thing to Farhaad. So I decided to call him. He picked up immediately.

Hey Angel. Already missing me? - He said in flirting manner but I rolled my eyes.

Can we meet? I want to talk to you about something. - I asked him.

Yes Ofcourse. I will come tonight. - He said and Before he could say anything I cuts the call. He calls me again but I immediately cuts his call again.

I was so much stressed right now, I need something to distract my mind so I decided to take shower. The warm water cascaded down my body washing away my worries. Suddenly I heard a door bell. I shouted to priya to open the door. I heard opening the door but couldn't listen further. I thought maybe Shazia or Alana had come.

I didn't pay that much attention, Suddenly I felt someone behind me. Before I could turned around, he put his hand on my mouth and I immediately realised who he was.

If I move my hand. Will you scream my Angel? - He asked in his husky voice in my ears. I rolled my eyes just by his breathing sensation on my neck. I nodded my head in No.

He moved my hand and turned me around. He was just in his jeans. He already took off his shirt. And God he was looking truly like a Devil. His deep black eyes was looking into my eyes like they want some answers. He was also getting wet in shower and his hairs are coming on his head. He sexily pushed his wet hairs back from his face to backwards. He looks so sexy and I was so fucking turned on just by looking at him.

Suddenly I realised that I was all naked in front of him. I tried to hide my breast with my hands but he slammed my hands forcefully on the wall. Then he came close to me and said.

Don't even try to hide your body from me again. - He said obsessively while looking at my breast and then again he looked deep in my eyes.

I didn't reply to him and he was confused now.

Why are you angry with me? Why were you not picking my calls? Did I do something wrong? - He asked like a little child and I smiled at him.

You tell me..Did you do something wrong that makes me angry? - I asked.

I haven't done anything wrong except seeing you naked here. - He said while bitting on my ear and I rolled my head backwards in sexually way.

God..Anushaa. Come to your senses...He's distracting you again. Stop itt. Just stop. - I yelled.

What happened? - He asked.

Why didn't you told me about the enmity between you and Kabir? - I asked and he was so shocked. He let go of my hands and took a step back and started rubbing his forehead.

Who told you? - He asked taking a deep breath.

Fortunately. Everybody knows that..except me.- I yelled.

Angel. Listen, I always wanted to told you but I was so afraid that you might leave me. - He said.

And won't I leave now? - I asked him.

He again pinned me to the wall and I can sensed his anger through his breathing.

You. Are. Not. Going. To. Leave. Me...UNDERSTAND!!!! You Are MINE!!! And if your fucking brother come between us, I swear to God Anushaa..I'm gonna Kill him without even thinking. He yelled while harshly gripped my mouth and I can see love care lust for me in those eyes.

He came close to me and his wet and slippery hands explored my body tracing the contours with a gentle touch. Our eyes met, spark ignited between us. Slowly our bodies drew closer. Our lips brushed against each other, a soft tentative touch that quickly turned into passionate kiss. Our tongue danced and explored, a symphony of wet desire.

As our kiss deepened, our bodies pressed together tightly. Then he started kissing me on my neck, he slowly started biting me. My moans filled the small space and he was groning on my neck.

He let go of my neck, look into my eyes for a second like he was asking me for permission, and I gave him by closing my eyes.

Farhaad POV-

I was so angry and confused when Anusha cuts my call. I was in the meeting with Jibraan, when she called. I left my meeting

in middle and raced to her house. I rang the door bell, her maid opened the door and she shivered while looking at me. I ignored her and asked.

Where is Anusha? - I asked.

Apne Kamree..me..hai.. - She said and I gently pushed her and go towards her room. She tried to stop me, I turned around and ask her to shut up and closed the door on her face. I looked in her room but she is nowhere suddenly I heard water following from her bathroom. She was in the shower and I smrinked at that thought. I took off my shirt and jumped into shower with her.

She was looking so divine when water flowes on her body through her curves and her ass. She looks like Goddess which I want to worship.

When she gave me that permission I again kissed her passion-ately, she moaned in my mouth and that makes me more horny for her. I grabbed her left boob and started pressing it. I took her pink erected nipple between my thumb and index finger and started pulling it gently. I let go off her lips and started sucking her other boob. It taste like honey, it feels like heaven. I slept with so many girls but no one made me feel that way.

You are so beautiful Angel. - I said while sucking her and she caressed my hairs with her hand and moaned. Her moaning makes me crazy. I want more. I want all of her.

I picked her up in my lap. She clung to me. I buried my face in her neck, she put her legs across my waist. Her cunt is rubbing against my stomach when I held her in my lap. And that makes me more crazy.

I got out of the bathroom with her in my lap and goes to her room. I threw her on bed and stood looking at her all whole naked wet body, her boobs were moving due to heavy breathing.

I licked my lips while looking at her and said-

Spread your legs for me,My Angel. I want to see what heaven looks and taste like.

- She bit and lips and spread her legs wide open for me. I went crazy. Goddd her pink pussy lips, her juices were flowing from her hole. I was no longer patient now. I got down on my knees for her. I grabbed her thighs and pulled her on the edge of the bed.

I started eating her cunt, it taste so damn good. It's feels like honey dripping from her cunt. I grabbed both of her boobs and pulled her nipples and played with them while eating her.

Her moans feels soothing song to my ears. She was not in her senses. I stood up and licked my lips while looking at her. I go towards her for kissing her lips.

Her hands were in my hair, pulling me even closer. Then I again grabbed her boobs and sucked them. And then kissed around her navel, her lower stomach and then again her pussy.

Stop please...stopp..no more..- She said while moaning heavily. I know she is about to cum. And I wanted to drink all her juices.

Ssshhh....just a little bit more.- I said and put my fingers inside her pussy forcefully. She moaned in pain. I started eating her and fingering her at same time. She was moaning so loudly. And when she's about to cum I stopped.

Whattt...fuckk..- She shouted in annoyance and anger.

Ofcourse Angel..we are about to.- I smrinked at her and her face turned scared from angry.

She bit her lips and looked deep in my eyes when I took off my pants. I again spread her legs and set myself in missionary position.

I put the tip of my dick at the opening of her pussy and pushed my dick slowly. I kissed her while giving her slow thrust. Slowly I increased my speed of thrusting her.

She felt like heaven to my hell, the closest I'd ever get to salvation. And yet I still wanted to drag her into the depths of hades with me.

I'm..your..enemy's....sisterr.. - she said while I am fucking her hard.

YOU *thrust* ARE *thrust* MINE *thrust* END OF DISCUS-SION

I said with anger and then we cummed together. I cummed into her and it's really feels what heaven feels like. I found my salvation deep between her legs.

Chapter 26

Kabir POV-

What? What the fuck are you saying? - Shazia yelled.

It's true. I saw marks on her body. And it's all my fault. I was so blinded by hatred that I didn't even think about whether she was safe or not. I said while putting my hand on forehand and felt so much hatred for myself.

I will go to her tomorrow and bring her back. - Shazia said.

I decided to go somewhere, I need fresh air. I called Imraan to come, we goes where we usually go. I told him everything that happened, I felt so much guilty. Imraan told me to calm down, but it was not working. The guilt in me was so much more than anything. I decided to go home, I drank alot. Imraan received a call from someone and then he left saying that it's something important. After drinking I goes to parking lot, I drank so much that my head was hurting, but that hatred inside me for myself, it's not gone.

When I started opening the door of my car, I heard some noise from behind. I turned around and saw four mens standing with weapons in their hands.

I'm already in bad mood. Not today!! - I said to them in annoyance and turned back to opening my car door.

No problem, everything will be alright soon.- one of them said.

Who sent you? - I asked while facing them.

Farhaad Mirza. - One of them said.

If I sent you, so Why don't I know about this? - familiar voice came from behind, I turned around to see who's that voice was.

It was Farhaad Mirza himself, sitting on the bonnet of his car. All four men got scared after seeing him. I was so drunk at that time that I can't stand by myself, so I sat on the ground, leaning my back against my car.

Farhaad took out his gun and I heard four gunshots, suddenly all four of them fell on the ground. Dead.

See, I told you. It was not me. - Farhaad said while sitting next to me on the ground.

If it's not you, then who the fuck wants to kill me? - I asked while rubbing my head in confusion.

You'll have to find that out as soon as possible. Whoever he is, ruined my name. He wants to start a fight between us. And one more thing, I won't come everytime to save you. And BTW you're welcome. - He said in sarcastic way.

I will. And Thankyou. - I said and when I stood up I fell down again because my head was spinning.

Let me drive you home. - Farhaad said.

Why the fuck you're helping me? And how do you I was here? - I asked him while he helped me in standing up.

I did a little research after you called me that night. And I know he will surely attack again. So I just kept an eye on you.- He said.

And I'm not helping you, he ruined my name. That's why I'm here. - He added.

He made me stand up and get me in his car. Then he drove me home. I didn't even realised when was I passed out.

Farhaad POV-

When Kabir called me that night, I felt something suspicious. If I didn't attack on him then who he was? And also he takes my name. He ruined my reputation. I have to take care of it. I called Jibraan and told him everything, I know he will attack again, that's why I kept eye on Kabir.

When he was all alone in that parking lot, four men came to killed him. But I saved him. I don't know why I did that. If he had died, it would have been better for me. Maybe I saved him because of My Angel. Godd..that girl. I can't get her out of mind since I fucked her. I want her more. Soon, I will.

I drove Kabir to his house, when we reached, I pulled him out of my car and supported him to stand up. I ranged the door bell and guess what?

My Angel opened the door, She was shocked while looking at me with Kabir. Kabir was not in his senses. I was about to tell her, suddenly Kabir's wife came and started worrying.

What happened to him? What did you do? - He asked me.

I did nothing. He drank alot, I drove him home. - I said and then he let's me in. I put Kabir on the couch and turned to Shazia.

Someone attacked him in the parking lot of club. He drank alot that he couldn't even stand by himself. - I said while looking at shazia and then my Angel. She was also so much scared.

Anusha told me what happened between Kabir and her that morning, that Kabir now realised his mistake. And how he wants to take her home. My anger subsided a little after listening all this.

Who attacked him? - Shazia asked in confusion.

I don't know but Kabir or I will find out soon. He taked my name in front of kabir, That I sent them. Whoever he was, runined my name too. I will not spare him. - I said in little anger.

Thankyou so much for saving him. - Anusha said. She knows that I saved him because of her.

Shazia went and sat beside Kabir. I nodded at Anusha and started leaving when Imraan, his friend came. He was so confused looking at me.

What happened? Is everything okay? - He asked while looking at shazia.

Why? Was something going to happen to him? - I asked with suspicious tone.

No..no.. I was just asking. - He stuttered while speaking.

Why are you here? How do you know he was here? - I asked him again.

I met him at the club, I got important call so I had to leave. I called him to ask if he reached home safe or not. When he didn't picked up my call, so I decided to come here. - He spokes as if he was explaining something.

And who are you to ask me these questions? I know you definitely done something to him. - He yelled at me.

Keep your voice down, Otherwise I'll cut your tongue. - I said threatening him.

Guys!!! Please stop. Farhaad, come with me. - Anusha came between us and pulled me outside the house.

She puts her soft hands on my cheek and touched her nose with mine.

Calmm down!!! Mr. Devil. Thankyouu for saving him. And sorry for What Imraan said.- she said softly. And godd, she has this power of controlling me.

I calmed down and pulled her into my arms and hugged her.

Take care of yourself too. If Kabir got attacked then you guys too can be attacked.- I said worriedly.

Don't worry. I have my Devil, who keeps all my demons away. - She whispered and I couldn't resist myself.

I kissed her. God, I needed that. I devoured her mouth with my tongue. She tried to free herself by pushing me on my chest. But I pulled her more closer. She tasted sweet like cotton candy.

Someone....will see us..leave me.. - she said against my mouth, while I kissing her.

So Am I scared of anyone? - I asked while letting her go.

You're not, but I am. - she said and started leaving inside the house.

Meet me tomorrow. On the beach. At 5pm.- I said to her and then she nodded yes and goes inside.

I was just started leaving, suddenly Imraan came from behind and again yelled.

I know it's you. You attacked him.- He said.

Not me. It's you. It's you Imraan, who attacked his best friend. I always had doubt on you. And you clearled my doubt my coming here. You came here to see if he was alive or not. - I said while turning my face towards him and he got scared and I caught him.

Kabir never gonna believe you.- He said while giving me devilish smile

Chapter 27

Farhaad POV-

I knew it. Imran was the one who attacked Kabir. But he's right, why would Kabir believe me? I have to do something.

Next day, I was going to meet Anusha, when I reached at beach, she was already there. Sitting on the ground, watching waves, warm sunlight felling on her angelic face and wind was blowing her hair. She's truly an Angel. But she looks dull.

Hey. - I said while sitting next to her.

She turned around to me and rest her head on my shoulder. It's was the most beautiful feeling for me.

What happened? Are you Okay? - I asked her.

Yes. I'm just little tired. - she replied.

How's kabir? - I asked.

He's fine. Told me alot about you. - She said and winks at me.

He would not have praised me. Right? - I asked.

Actually he did. He told me how you saved him. And Thankyouu again for saving him. - She said while looking at me and stood up.

Anusha I think I know who tried to kill your brother. - I said to her randomly. And also I didn't want her to put herself in danger so she has to know.

What? Who? - She asked in confusion.

Imraan. Your brother's best friend. Last night, he was acting all weird. Like he was there to see that if Kabir died or not. And after you go inside, I threatened him to tell Kabir all this but he said that Kabir never gonna believe me. - I told her everything and she got scared.

Maybe you should tell Kabir all this. Last night, you saved him. He's gonna believe you. - she replied while patting my arm.

I will. - I said to her.

Let's take a walk. - She said.

I stood up and started walking behind her holding her hands. We were laughing, giggling and talking.I never thought that I could have her on my side.She goes into water and started playing with it. I stood a little distance away from her and looked at her and thinking that.

One day, and I mean soon. I'm going to make this women my Wife, My partner.My everything.She'll be my always and I'll be hers.Forever.

And I made promise to myself that nobody in this fucking world is not going to hurt her. I'm gonna give her my all love and care. She deserves all of it.

She came back to me and I hugged her tightly.

What good deed did this Devil do, that I found you. And now you are mine.-I asked her and she went away from my arms while blushing.

But when she turned away, she bumped into someone. And he was none other than Kabir malik, her brother. He was standing with Imraan who was looking at me. And I know he told Kabir about us.

She looked at her with anger and then he grabbed her hand and started taking her away from me.

Kabir stop. - I yelled.

Take her in the car. - Kabir said to Imran. And when he touched her. My blood boiled in anger. She tries to get away from him, but Imran was leaving her hand and then he forcefully pulled her towards the car.

I tried to reach to her. But Kabir stopped me.

Stay away from her. - He said while pointing his finger towards me and then he turned away and started leaving.

I love your sister. - I said to him, then he turned around and punched me across the face. I fell on ground. Next thing I saw that Anusha was sitting behind in the car and crying, Imraan smrinked at me. I swear I'm gonna kill that bastard.

Anusha POV-

It was all going well. I was so happy now that my brother is doing great. Everything in my life was back on track now. But my happiness won't last forever.

Kabir saw me with Farhaad, he told Imraan to get me into the car. He dragged me harshly to the car and made me sat on the backseat.

I saw Farhaad and Kabir talking but suddenly Kabir punched him. I thought that Farhaad might hit kabir but he didn't. I know he's enduring all this because of me.

Kabir sat on the front seat and Imraan drove the car. I tried talking to Kabir but he didn't listen to me. He was ignoring me all the way to home.

When we reached home, he dragged me inside. Shazia was there in the hall and stood up while watching us.

What happened? Whay the hell are you dragging her? - Shazia yelled.

Ask her. What the hell she was doing with that Farhaad? Since when was all this going on? - He asksd turning towards me.

I love him. - I said while crying.

Kabir raised his hand to slap me but shazia stopped him.

I will take care of her. Please just let me talk to her. - Shazia said while taking me to the room.

When we goes inside, she closed the door and make me sit on bed and stand in front of me, folding her hands.

What happened? Farhaad? How did you even meet him? - She asked lots of questions.

I told her how we met and everything. And told her how much I love him.

Anusha, you know about their enmity. Then why? -she asked.

Because it was too late when I found out. - I said.

Kabir will never be happy. But I'm always with you.She said while hugging me.

Suddenly the door opened widely and Kabir came in with anger.

Give me your phone and Listen Shazia, she won't leave this house. - he angrily while snatching my phone.

And you, remove that Farhaad from your mind. He tried to kill me twice.- He said to me angrily.

But I love him. And he saved you. He's not your enemy. He didn't attacked you.- I said to him.

Then who did? I don't have any other enemy other than him. - he said.

Farhaad told me that it was Imraan who tried to killed you. He confessed last night in front of him. - I said bluntly.

Enough!!! It's just too much now. You believed that bastard. Aree he was using you. - he said in frustration.

This was really too much for me. We fought alot on this topic. Imraan was right, Kabir never gonna believe us. The head started spinning, I think I'm again having panic attack. I didn't realised when I passed out. And the next thing is that I opened my eyes in the hospital room.

Chapter 28

Anusha POV-

When I opened my eyes, I saw Kabir and Shazia sitting next to my hospital bed. I sat and my brain was throbbing in my head.

What happened? - I looked at Kabir while rubbing my forehead and he gave me that angry expressions.

Anusha, you need to lay down. - Shazia said while standing up.

What happened? Why I'm here? - I asked again and refused to lay down.

You fainted last night. So we bought you to the hospital. - Kabir said while standing up and everybody stays silent.

Is there anything you guys aren't telling me? - I asked them with confusion.

No. Nothing. - Kabir said turning his face towards me.

Kabir, she has a right to know. - Shazia yelled and then she sat next to me.

Anusha, You are pregnant. - She said and my jaw dropped in fear. How can this happen?

Then I suddenly remembered what happened between me and Farhaad. Oh God, This is his baby. And then I remembered that zayn always kept me on birth control, since I came here I stopped taking birth control pills.

What have I done? Kabir must be thinking so bad about me and then tears fell down from my eyes.

I told you. I told you Anusha, stay away from him. But no, you found only that person to love in the whole world. He fucking used you Anusha. - He yelled at me and I cried looking at him.

It's not too late yet. You will abort this baby. - He said and it felt like the ground slipped beneath my feet.

No. First I want to meet Farhaad. It's his baby. He also has a right to know.- I said while standing up from the bed.

Are you crazy? He will never gonna accept this baby.I'm going to tell the doctor that we are ready for abortion process. - He said and left from the room.

I tried going behind him but I was so weak that I fell down. Shazia put me up and sat me down on the bed.

Please Shazia, help me.. stop him. And please call Farhaad. - I begged her.

Anusha, I can't. If kabir got to know, he will kill me.- she said.

Please help me..helppp.- I again get unconscious.

Farhaad POV-

I am missing her so much right now. I wish I could stop Kabir from taking her away from me. But I know anusha loves her brother so much. That's why I didn't do anything. But I want her, I need her.

Suddenly my phone rang, it was an unknown number. And when I picked I was shocked listening to the voice. It was Shazia, Kabir's wife.

Farhaad, I don't have time. Just come to K.C. Hospital. - she said in hurry.

What? What happened? Is Anusha okay? - I said anxiously.

No she's not. She fainted last night. We bought her to the hospital. And then we found out that.... she stopped talking in middle and suddenly I heard a manly voice.

Maybe It was Kabir, he snatched her phone and when I tried again it was switched off. Something is very very wrong. I hurriedly sat in my car and raced to the hospital. I also called Jibraan to come with me.

Why my Angel is in hospital? Did Kabir hurt her? I'm gonna kill that bastard if he did something to her. I reached there as fast as I can.

I reached to the reception and asked the receptionist about Anusha. She gave me the room number and directions.

When I reached, Kabir was standing outside the room, and he got shocked when he looked at me.I go to him and grabbed his collar in anger.

Where's my Anusha? What did you do to her? - I yelled at him while he tried to remove my hands.

I did nothing. And I told you stay away from my sister. - He yelled.

Sister? Suddenly you started worrying a lot about her. Where did this love go when that man raped her everyday? - I asked him in while grinding my teeth.

He pushed me and tried to punched me again. But not this time. I dodged his punch and again grabbed him by his throat.

I'm asking you one last time. Where is Anusha? - I asked in anger.

I..did..nothing. - He said with difficulty in breathing.

Where is she? - I again yelled.

Suddenly shazia came running from the hall towards us. She looked so worried and feared about something. Kabir pushed me and goes to her.

What happened Shazia? I told you to stay with Anusha. Where is she? - kabir asked.

Anusha...anushaa..she's is not in the operation theatre. Doctor asked me to bring some medicines. I go downstairs for just 5 minutes. And when I came upstairs, I heard some weird noises.S uddenly nurse came from inside. She told me that Someone killed the doctor who's operating her. Someone kidnapped Anusha.- she said while breathing so fast.

Whatt?? Why was she is in the operation room? Can anybody tell me something? Damnnitt!!! - I yelled again.

Last night, she fainted when we were fighting about you. I thought that it was stress, that's why she fainted but when we bought her to the hospital, we found out that...that she..she is pregnant.Kabir said and I didn't understand how to react. How did this happen? I was so happy and emotional.I can't describe my feelings.

And why was she is in the operation room? - I asked with anger in my eyes.

Because she was getting abortion.- He replied and I took out of my gun and placed the gun on his head.

You were going to kill my baby? How did you even dare ?- I asked in anger but shazia came between us.

This is not the time to fight amongst ourselves. They kidnapped her. And abortion did not happened. She's still pregnant. - Shazia said and I let go of Kabir.

Who the fuck kidnapped her, if it's not you? -Kabir asked.

I know. It was your best friend, Imraan. He's the one who attacked you twice taking my name. And now when his attack was not successful, he kidnapped Anusha.- I said in frustration.

No, that's not true. He can't do this. - Kabir said.

Oh really? Then where is he now? - I said in sarcastic way.

We were fighting but suddenly Kabir's phone beeped. It was a video message from Anusha's number. When he opened the video, he fell down on the floor and started crying, I immediately picked his phone from the ground and opened the video.My blood boiled in anger, that motherfucker will now gonna know that why do they call me devil.

Chapter 29

Farhaad POV-

I told Jibraan to find the location of this video. That bastard touched my angel and my baby. Now that bastard gonna pay the price for what he did.

In that video Anusha was tied to a chair unconscious. And that bastard was touching her neck with his fingers. I'm gonna cut those fingers and then I'll feed him his fingers.

How could I be such a bad brother? I couldn't save her before nor could I save her now. - Kabir said while crying on the floor.

What is the use of regretting now? Call that bastard and ask him what the fuckk he want? - I said to kabir and then he pull out his phone and called imraan.

I asked him to put the phone on speaker. He picked up after few rings.

It took you too long to call. Maybe you don't love your sister.- He said while laughing.

You were my best friend. Why are you doing this? - Kabir asked.

When I first saw her, I fell in love with her. I tried to tell you so many times. But I know you won't let me come near her. So I tried to kill you, after that I marry Anusha and your company would also become mine. - He said.

But this bitch, she went to Farhaad for a fuck. This bitch made my job more difficult. That's why my mens took Farhaad's name while attacking you.So that you fight amongst yourselves and one of you dies.But I don't know where the love between you two came from, I tried to provoke Kabir alot. But he didn't do anything. Now there's one way left, kidnap her and make her mine. Forcefully or by her wish.

He said and before I could say anything he cuts the call and switched off his phone.God..I haven't asked anything before today but now I'm begging you, save my Anusha and my baby.

Anusha POV-

When I opened my eyes, my head was paining alot. I saw around me, this is not the hospital. This is some room with dim lights. I can't tell where I am right now. Suddenly I felt pain in my wrists and ankles. Then I realised I'm tied to a chair.

Helpp...Bhaiijaan..Shaziaaa..Helppp. - I yelled.

Suddenly the door opened wide and a manly figure come near me. I can't see his face in dim light. But he laughed when I was struggling.

No one is here to help you. It's just you and me Babydoll. - He said.

That name. Babydoll. For once I thought that it was zayn. I started struggling and crying loudly. If the same thing happens to me again, I might not survive this time.

He switched on the lights. My eyes took a while to adjust. When my eyes opened, I saw Imraan standing in front of me.

Youu. You were my brother's best friend. How could you did this to him? - I yelled.

He put both his hands on my hands which were tied to the chair and leaned before my face.

If a friend's sister is so beautiful, then anybody can do this to his best friend. - He said near my lips and then he goes towards my neck and started kissing and bitting. I tried to struggle but I was tied, so I couldn't do anything.I was missing Farhaad so much right now, He wouldn't let that happen to me. He doesn't even know where I am. Nor does he know that I'm pregnant with his baby.Oh God, my baby. Please save us Farhaad.

Suddenly he started tearing my hospital gown, which   Doctor gave me to wear before operation.

If Farhaad comes to know about this, He will kill you. - I yelled while spitting on him.

He stood up straight and cleaned his face. And then he slapped me across my face, I fell down tied with that chair. And then I feel blood in my mouth.

By the time he comes, I would have done everything with you. I'm gonna fuck you hard that you can't walk for weeks. - He said while sitting down on his knees beside me.And then he picked me up, opened my arms and pull me up and then he threw me on the bed. I started to slide backwards but he grabbed my leg and pulled me towards him.Then he tighly grabbed my both arms and tied them with headboard of the bed with rope.

Now where will you go? - He said while laughing.

Please..please leave me. I'm pregnant.- I said while begging him.

What? Pregnant? Whose baby is this? - He asked in confusion.

Farhaad. - I said while crying.

Then It will be lot of fun, when I take this child out of your belly and send it to Farhaad. - He said while laughing.

I was so scared when he said those filthy words, but now I knew that I wouldn't be able to survive. Only thing that I can do is pray, pray for some miracle.

Please Farhaad. Save us. God please.. Farhaad. - I whispered to myself.

He again leaned over me and tear my hospital gown. I was half naked in front of him. Then he grabbed my one breast harshly and took other breast in his mouth and started sucking it.

Now I know why Farhaad is so crazy about you. You taste like heaven. - He said while smriking and again started sucking hardly on my neck and breast.

Then I thought that If I have to die, this time I will die fighting and not in fear. My legs were not tied, when he stood up again to spread my legs, I kicked him. I kicked him with my leg on his dick.He screamed in pain and then he move backwards. I again started struggle, the rope was tied loose. I was successfully opened the rope and stood up from the bed and started running towards the door.

When I opened the door I saw two figures standing with guns in their hands. It was Kabir and Farhaad, I was very happy to see them both. I tried to go towards them, but suddenly Imraan pulled me back and put knife on my stomach.

Don't come forward, otherwise I will kill both your child and your sister. - He said while looking at them and again put knife on my stomach.

If anything happens to her, I will torture you so much that you will beg for your death. - Farhaad said in anger and put his gun towards him.

If you take one step forward, I'll kill her. - Imraan said, Kabir takes one step closer.

Please leave her, I'm begging you. Take whatever you want, but leave her. Please. - Kabir said.

So you guy's won't stop like this. If I die I'll take her with me. - He said and stabbed my stomach with that knife.

I felt blood on my stomach and on my hands. I looked at Farhaad, he pulled the trigger and then I heard a gunshot, that bullet hit imraan. We both fell down, I remembered Kabir and Farhaad pulled me towards them. I felt my eyes closing, I placed my bloody hand on Farhaad's face and said -

Sa..save..your...Baby.

And then my eyes closed and there's was darkness all around.

Chapter 30

Farhaad POV-

I was waiting for Jibraan to send me the location, the more time went by, the scared I become. Today for the first time, I was afraid of loosing someone. I don't know which state she would be in. I can't loose her.

Suddenly my phone rang, It was Jibraan. He send me the location of Anusha, I told the location to Kabir. Kabir said that it's the location of Imraan's second house. We both sat in the car and I raced as fast as I can.

When we reached there, the place seems abandoned. I called Jibraan again to ask if this is the right location. He said that I was at right place.We decided to go inside. The main door was closed from inside, we go backside of the house and luckily there's window which was opened. We both jumped inside.

Suddenly I heard my Angel screaming, that bastad was hurting her. We go upstairs running, I opened the door, my Angel was standing there, I tried to hold her hand but Imraan suddenly pulled her from me.

Then he stabbed in her stomach. I felt like my soul left my body for a second. But when Anusha fell on the floor, I pulled the trigger. The bullet hits his shoulder and then he also fell. I pulled Anusha in my arms, and her last words scared me like hell. For a minute I thought that I lost her.

Take her to the hospital and I'm gonna take care of that bastard. - Kabir said.

Call Jibraan from my phone. He'll help you. - I said to kabir while pulled out my phone and gave it to him.

I picked Anusha up in my arms and ran towards my car, then put her in the backseat and raced to the hospital.

Please God please..Save her. Please - I was praying to the God, I was doing something which I never did. But to save her, I can beg to anybody.

We reached hospital, I again picked her up in my arms and took her inside. Doctor immediately came for help. They put Anusha on the stretcher and directly took her in the operation theater. She was unconscious, and was not opening her eyes. I was scared to death. I saw myself in the window mirror, All my clothes were soaked in Anusha's blood. But soon, Anusha's blood will be replaced by Imraan's blood.After sometime, Kabir came.

Where is she? What did doctor said? - Kabir asked me anxiously.

I don't know. She is in the operation room. - I said.

Where is Imraan? Is he dead? - I asked Kabir.

No he's not dead. Jibraan took him to your place. - He said.

Anusha was in the operation room for 2 hours, and in that time I thought atleast 200 ways of torture for Imraan.

After 2 hours, doctor came outside. We both immediately go to him and asked.

How is she? Is she okay? - I asked.

There is nothing to worry about. She is fine. - Doctor said.

And I felt relieved after hearing this. I literally hugged Kabir. God listened to me. I got so much emotional that tears fell from my eyes.

But.. there is bad news. - Doctor said again.

What happened? - Kabir asked.

We couldn't save the baby. The knife hit the baby directly. - Doctor said and my happy tears convert into sad tears and anger.

I fell on the ground, holding my head.

I couldn't save my child. It's all my fault. - I cried in the arms of kabir.

Can we meet her? - Kabir asked.

No. She's is unconscious, she need rest. You can meet her tomorrow. - Doctor said and left from there.

Now my anger was on cloud 9, I'm gonna kill that bastard. He killed my baby, put the life of my Angel in danger. He has to pay the price for it.

You stay here with Anusha, I'll be back. - I said to Kabir.

I sat down in my car, then I called Jibraan. He put that bastard in my warehouse. I raced there as fast as I can.

When I reached there, I saw him unconscious tied on the chair. I rolled my sleeves up and open first two buttons of my shirt. I poured water on him. He immediately got his consciousness.

Where am I? - He asked.

Oh boy!! You are on the way to hell. - Jibran said while laughing.

Ready for the punishment? - I asked him.

Leave me..please..I made a mistake..sorry..please leave me. - He begged while crying in fear.

Mistake?? YOU KILLED MY BABY!!!!! You put her life in danger. - I screamed and he got more scared.

Sorry please...leave me..sorry. - He begged.

This is my favourite part..when people begged to me in fear. I loved that alot. - I said while picking up a knife from the table.

You touched her with same fingers, Right? - I said while holding his wrist.

No..No..leave me..pleea...- Before he could say anything, I cut off his fingers. He screamed in pain. And this pain is like a soothing song for me.I again grabbed his other hand and chopped off his other fingers too.

Then I sliced the knife on his shoulder, where the bullet hits before. He again screamed. I slowly put the knife into the wound and pull out fastly.

I stabbed the same spot 20 times with a knife. He was bleeding and soaked in his own blood. And then I grabbed his hands and sliced his veins of both of his hand. And left him for slow painful death.

Dump his body, when he dies, I need to go back to Anusha. - I said to Jibraan and left from there.

Next day, Anusha gained her consciousness. Kabir and me already sitting next to Anusha. When she opened her eyes, I hold her hand, and then she started crying while looking at us.

He killed my baby. - She said while crying.

I got up and kissed her forehead. And caressed her hair with my hand.

It's okay Angel. Now I'm here with you. I promise I'm never gonna leave you alone. And for that, If I have to kill you brother, I will kill him.- I said while kissing her again.

Excuse me, I'm right here..- kabir said with annoyance and then we all laughed.

Epilogue

A nusha POV-

Today is our 1 year anniversary, Farhaad and I got married when I came back from the hospital. He didn't want to be away from me for even a minute.I was so disturbed because of that incident and still having nightmares of that day, but this time I was not alone, I have my whole family who is taking care of me. My Husband, My brother and my Sister-in-law.

One good thing happened from this incident, Farhaad and Kabir became friends. They still have their differences but they are working on it.

I was getting ready, Farhaad is going to take me on a date. I was sitting in front of the dressing table. He came from behind and put both of his hands on my shoulder and kissed my head.

My heart still skiped a beat, while looking at you.- He whispered and I blushed.

Then he took out something from his pocket, it was a ring box. Then he turned my chair around and sit on his knees.

For you, My Angel.- He said and then he put the ring on my finger.

I have a gift for you too. - I said and then I turned around and picked the box from the table and handed that box to him.

He opened the box and looked at it in confusion. I laughed looking at his face.

It's a...its..a pregnancy test. Oh god...Are you..Are pregnant? - He said and I laughed looking at him.He was giggling like a baby.

Yes. Mr. Farhaad Mirza..you are going to be a father.I said and then he stood up and picked me up in his arms. Then he took me to the bed and put me down slowly, he came over me and kissed me so deep. This kiss is same as when he kissed me first time. Full of love, care and little bit of lust.

I promise Angel, I will take care of you and our baby. I will place the happiness of the whole world at your feet. Nobody gonna come between us. - He whispered and again kissed me while putting his hands on my belly.

I never imagined that my life could be like this. Maybe I'm the most lucky girl in the world.